DOCTOR WHO

ANNUAL 1981

£1.95

COLONY OF DEATH

The television screen flickered, the signal seeming to battle its way through a plethora of electronic garble before reforming as a recognisable picture. The man watching darted an angry foot towards it, striking it hard on one side, but the machine took no notice and continued its barely decipherable message.

"I've told you before, Havard," intoned a woman's voice from the next room, "it's no good taking it out on the machines. Everybody's is the same these days. There's so much electronic noise cramming the air waves that they're overloaded."

"That don't stop me getting angry, Heleen," grunted Havard. "I pays my taxes—the machine gotta work proper if I pays for it. Some time I get so sickful of this planet. Nothing work good no more."

Havard slumped back in his plasti-seat, forehead screwed up with intense concentration as he tried to follow the programme. Heleen entered, two small trays in her hands. She gave one to Havard and sat on the only other seat there was space for in the cramped room.

"Not this garbage more!" yelled Havard, his temper thoroughly roused. "I sickful of this foods, this teevee, and the whole rotten planet by golly! Everything no good now, no room for live, no nothing. Pretty soon too much people and no much air. I sickful, Heleen, I tells you."

Heleen knew and agreed. She nodded but said nothing. The TV spluttered and the picture cleared a little.

A spacious, airy, urban landscape of graceful, slender buildings swum on to the screen and a smiling figure stepped up to the camera.

"Ever seen anything like this, folks? In the history books maybe, or a painting somewhere. Well, let me assure you good people that what you're seeing is real enough . . ." The camera panned out to show a small family group playing ball together on some parkland, flanked by pleasant, clean-looking villas. " . . . this is the land of plenty—and that means plenty of everything for everybody. Space, fresh air, clean water, large and modern apartments—the list is endless." The camera cut to a close-up of his face. "And where, you are asking, is this paradise? Not on Earth, surely. No friends, this is a colony belonging to New Worlds Incorporated, and for the amazing price of 5 million dolas you and your family could join us here tomorrow. Hurry to your New Worlds Travel Office in your mega-city today, and start a new life in Paradise with us."

Havard sat bolt upright, his eyes bulging.

"By golly, Heleen, I am enough here on Earth. We go to Paradise, yes?"

"Sure, Havard, but where do we get 5 million dolas?"

"I rob a bank, anything, you bet. Me, you, the kids, we go to Paradise tomorrow, by golly okay!"

Romana drew her head out from underneath one of the banks of instruments, looking perturbed.

"I'm worried about this omni-directional impulse stabiliser Doctor."

The Doctor peered into the maze of circuitry.

"The omni-directional . . . oh well, I shouldn't bother too much about that, Romana. Just talk to it nicely," he announced authoritatively.

"Don't you ever read your operational manual, Doctor?" asked Romana, not to be put off. "Don't tell me—you've seen it all and done it all before."

"How did you guess?" smiled the Doctor.

Romana remained unmistakably concerned. "I'm serious, Doctor," she stated firmly. "It's functioning much too erratically for safety's sake and if it malfunctions during flight—"

"Ah, yes!" The Doctor shut his eyes tight, clapped his hand over his brow and began pacing up and down. "It's all coming back to me now. Er . . . omni-directional stabiliser . . . er . . . malfunction . . . er. Good Lord! Do you realise, if it malfunctions during flight we'll materialise wherever we are—"

"Inside out," said Romana, patiently. "Yes, I know."

Romana's words fell on deaf ears as the Doctor strode over to the control console, his fingers working rapid patterns over the array of buttons.

"What **are** you doing, Doctor?"

"Landing, what else? replied the Doctor, tersely. "You may

know your theory, Romana, but when it comes to an emergency, we old hands, you know, we . . ." His voice trailed off as he concentrated on the controls.

After a few moments he stepped back, satisfied.

"There, that should do it—I've turned the control console over to automatic with instructions to land us at the nearest available point in space and time with a level twelve technology rating. I should be able to cobble a few odds and ends together from whatever they have, to make a new unit." The Doctor flashed a smile at Romana, and leant nonchalantly against the console.

"But Doctor, you'll overload—"

"Nonsense! This old girl was built to withstand—"

The **Tardis** suddenly shuddered violently, the lights dimming and fading as the Doctor and Romana were thrown off their feet. For what seemed ages, the very fabric of the **Tardis** seemed to threaten to tear itself apart, until eventually the shaking subsided and slowed to a standstill.

The Doctor looked up and dusted himself off.

"I admit I've made better landings, but we **have** landed—and the right way out," he beamed. "I wonder where we are—the instruments don't seem to be registering."

Romana shook her head and said, "You've burnt the unit out altogether, and it's affected the main circuits. We're stuck here."

The Doctor hung his head in mock sadness. "Oh, don't be such a pessimist. What better incentive to find a new one? Where's your sense of adventure?" He extracted the damaged unit, dropped it in his pocket, and walked jauntily to the door. "Well, what are we waiting for? If we don't hurry, all the shops will be closed!"

An unnatural silence greeted the Doctor as he stepped through the **Tardis** door and stood gazing at what appeared to be a deserted city street. Romana and K-9 joined him, and they surveyed the scene with interest.

"It looks like the planet Earth, Doctor," opined Romana.

"Yes," agreed the Doctor. "The style of architecture suggests late 23rd century, but there's something not quite right about it. Have you noticed?"

Romana took in the broad, sweeping street and graceful, slender buildings that adorned it. Along the street she could see a park and beyond it clean-lined, modern villas. "It's so silent," she said at last.

"So silent it's unreal—and not a person in sight even though it's broad daylight." The Doctor took a few exploratory steps down the street and cupped his hands to his mouth. "Hallo-o! Any-body-home?!"

His voice echoed emptily round the towering blocks . . . but no answer came. "Perhaps it's half-day closing. Let's go and investigate. There's a police station over there—there's sure to be somebody on duty."

The Doctor reached the door of the police station and pushed it open. He disappeared momentarily and reappeared with a look of astonishment on his face.

"You're not going to believe this, Romana . . . not only are there no policemen in there, but also no police station either," explained the Doctor, scratching his head.

Romana moved past him and looked through the door. Behind it lay a flat, empty landscape, a block of buildings visible on the

horizon, some distance away. She turned to the Doctor questioningly.

The Doctor knelt to speak to K-9. "I'm right in assuming, K-9, that this is not, in fact, the planet Earth at the end of the 23rd century, am I not?"

"Affirmative, Master," replied K-9. "Atmospheric conditions and the absence of humans suggest, contrary to appearances, that we are not on the planet Earth."

"What K-9's actually saying," continued the Doctor, "is that, according to Earth history, we ought to be in a city that's packed to the seams with people and polluted to an excessive level—which as you can see, we're very evidently not. Any ideas, K-9?"

K-9's antennae revolved while he monitored some readings.

"My sensors indicate a major power source directly ahead, Master. Traces of animate life forms also evident."

The Doctor gazed towards the distant complex of buildings. "I really must get that computer to pay more attention to where it lands. Best wheel forward, K-9. Lead on!"

The buildings had looked deceptively close but it was almost an hour later before the three companions finally reached them. The Doctor set a brisk pace across the enormous, open plain, and arriving at their destination, Romana slumped down on a wall and proceeded to rub her tired feet.

"I'm exhausted, Doctor," she said. "Can we rest a moment?"

"I'll go and look round. You stay with Romana, K-9," ordered the Doctor and, adjusting his scarf, he headed off towards the complex.

The buildings were windowless and doorless, so he followed the line of the wall to the corner. The building led away into the distance, the same featureless appearance suggesting little hope of an entrance. Undeterred, the Doctor proceeded to the next corner and, turning it, stopped dead in amazement.

A massive compound, bordered by a high wire fence, met his gaze; it too was empty, but a gate in it faced a single set of doors into the building, and the Doctor made straight for them.

He had barely reached them when two uniformed figures burst out, hand blasters trained menacingly at him.

"Ah, good day, gentlemen," the Doctor began cheerily. "I wonder if—"

The figures seized him by his arms and pulled him inside, bundling their captive down a maze of corridors, before abruptly turning into an office.

It was simply furnished, with a small bedroom off to one side. An imposing character in his fifties, a shock of white hair topping strong, set features, sat at a large desk, facing him. A considerable number of blueprints and star charts lined the walls. The Doctor was dumped in a chair, and the uniformed figures withdrew to stand guard by the door.

"We found the man, Garderon," one of them announced.

"I'm the Doctor. Nice of you to see me without an appointment," grinned the Doctor, amiably. "Of course, if you're busy, I can call back tomorrow." He rose as if to leave, but was halted by Garderon's booming command.

"Sit down at once, and keep your mouth firmly shut until I ask you to speak." Garderon toyed with a pen and tapped it slowly but firmly on the desk while carefully scrutinising the Doctor. At length, he meticulously replaced the pen in its desk stand, and leant forward, hands clasped together.

"You are trespassing on company property. What are you doing here? Answer!" he demanded, fixing the Doctor in a steely gaze.

The Doctor sat relaxed in his chair.

"Oh, just a flying visit," he said airily. "I was passing by and thought I'd drop in to see if you have one or two electronic components I could use to repair my ship."

Garderon flashed a glance at the uniformed men.

"Any reports of a ship landing?" They shook their heads in unison, and he turned back to the Doctor. "It is impossible to land inside the Dome without going through the entrance lock."

"A dome? That would explain the artificial sunlight and the controlled climate," said the Doctor, half to himself.

Garderon slammed a fist on the desk. "Stop playing games with me . . . Doctor, or whatever your name is. Who sent you here to spy on us?"

"Me, a spy?" laughed the Doctor. "By the way, what planet is this, if you don't mind me asking?"

Garderon snorted angrily and rose to his feet. "It's no use trying to bluff your way out of it. There are only two sets of people on this planet—my staff and the workers—and you are evidently from neither. Besides," he continued, pacing away from the desk, "you know very well where you are."

"Remind me," answered the Doctor, "I forget."

Garderon swung round viciously and advanced on the Doctor. "We are on the planet Paradise I, and **you** are here illegally!"

"Really?" replied the Doctor. "I always thought Paradise was supposed to be a green and pleasant land, all sunshine and smiles."

Garderon raised a fist to strike, but was interrupted by a buzz from his intercom. He flicked the switch down with irritation.

"Yes?" he snapped.

"New intake arriving from Earth on landing pads, Garderon. Better prepare reception," said the disembodied voice.

Garderon barked an acknowledgement into the intercom and glared at the Doctor.

"Take this man to the reception room. He can join the new work force once they're reanimated," he commanded. "We will talk again, Doctor."

“Cryogenic freezing? Suspended animation on their journey from Earth, I suppose,” said the Doctor. He smiled wickedly. “Now, I wonder why?”

“Take him away!” shouted Garderon.

The men moved forward and a sudden crushing blow to the back of the Doctor’s head sent the blood singing in his ears, and the world dissolved into blackness.

Romana woke with a start from her doze to find K-9 nudging her leg.

“Wake up, Mistress. I think we should retire to a place of safety. Sensors indicate spacecraft imminently descending in this immediate vicinity.”

They immediately took shelter, and watched in fascination as three enormous spacecraft came in to land on the open plain they had recently crossed.

Once landing was completed, several small trucks appeared from round the corner of the building, pulling long trains of trailers. They approached the spacecraft, which opened up like giant mouths. Dozens of humans, dressed in ragged clothes and looking emaciated, tramped across to the waiting trucks and, goaded on by armed guards, began loading a procession of long, transparent boxes on to the trailers.

“Coffins?” mused Romana, thinking aloud.

“Correction, Mistress. Readings indicate a large number of living humans, artificially frozen in suspended animation—as in the transport of inter-stellar colonists.”

“There are certainly enough of them. I don’t like the look of those armed guards though—I think we’ll stay undercover until it’s quieter before we try to find out what’s happening. I wonder what can be taking the Doctor so long? I do hope he’s safe.”

The Doctor looked up bleary-eyed, and felt a throbbing pain at the back of his skull. He eased himself up gently and peered round curiously.

He was lying in a low-ceilinged room of gigantic proportions, rather like a factory. Transparent, cryogenic freeze units, in piles of four, were stacked in all directions. By the signs of life they were showing it was evident that the reanimation process was almost complete. Already, small groups were being herded by the guards through some doors at the far end, too confused and disorganised to offer much resistance.

“Come on, you, join the others,” growled a rough voice and the Doctor found himself herded along into the growing streams of people being fed through the doors.

It was not long before they emerged through the opening opposite the compound, and were thrown inside by the guards. The Doctor scanned the frightened faces of the men, women and children as they stood dazed, uncomprehending.

As the artificial day drew to its unnatural close, the regular shifts of underground workers were returned to the wire enclosure. Haggard and drawn, some barely able to stand, they stumbled through the gates and collapsed exhausted in the nearest available space.

The Doctor watched them keenly and finally picked out a

small group who looked reasonably able to answer his questions. He introduced himself, and soon had two of them deep in conversation.

"It was a trap, you see, Doctor," said Starlis, the older of the two. "They lured us here with promises of a new world, free from overpopulation and pollution, guaranteed us work and accommodation—"

"And this is it," said Micra, a pretty blonde girl who had arrived on the last colony transporter. "Most don't last too long. The mining soon exhausts the workers, and if you don't die from overwork or starvation, the futility of the situation soon breaks your spirit."

"It's a perfect crime, Doctor," continued Starlis. "We think Garderon must have stumbled on this place by accident—as far as we can discover it's probably some minor moon actually within the solar system."

"I guessed as much from the star charts in his office," said the Doctor, nodding agreement. "So Garderon finds this place, rich in minerals, and decides to equip himself with a cheap labour force by tricking people into believing that they're escaping to some distant planet in deep space."

"On top of that," added Micra, "he finances his mining equipment and space fleet by charging us all five million dolas for the privilege of becoming his slaves."

The Doctor looked serious. "It's a devilish plan. How is it nobody on Earth has realised any of this? Surely you have relatives back home?"

Starlis answered tight-lipped. "In the first week or two of arrival, Garderon and his henchmen will take samples of handwriting from all of you. We all had to fill in extremely detailed forms before we came so he has a full dossier on each one of us. He just feeds the sample and the biographical details into the computer and composes imaginary letters for the people back home on Earth."

"Clever," admitted the Doctor. "How does he explain why no one ever goes back?"

"Have you ever seen 23rd century New York, Doctor?" asked Micra.

"Not recently."

"Well, believe me, if this place was as good as it's advertised to be, there wouldn't be any question of choice. Nobody lives on Earth these days if they can afford not to."

The Doctor hummed to himself and his eyes opened wide as an idea struck him. "It seems to me," he began, "that a few domes like this set up around this moon could make this place ideal for a col-

ony—a self-supporting one at that, if the mineral deposits are as rich as Garderon seems to think."

"That's all very well," moaned Micra, despondently, "but we're inside a cage—weak, hungry and unarmed."

"Never say die, Micra," enthused the Doctor, "I have a feeling the cavalry may yet arrive."

K-9 trundled through the semi-darkness, Romana close behind him.

"The Doctor is nearby, Mistress. I have located him by homing in on the damaged unit he carries with him," intoned K-9.

Romana pulled K-9 to a halt as they rounded the building and the compound came into view. Timing it so that they avoided the patrolling guards, they soon located the Doctor, and K-9 made short work of the fence, burning a hole large enough to climb through.

"Start passing the word, Starlis. A small group of you should be able to deal with the guards—they won't be expecting trouble."

"What are you going to do, Doctor?"

"Garderon and I have a little chat to finish."

The Doctor gave a quiet chuckle, and they set off along the compound perimeter. K-9 stunned the only guard they met, and forced an entrance through the main doors to the control complex. The Doctor led them through the labyrinth of corridors to Garderon's quarters, recalling his earlier, forced trip.

"Guard this door, K-9. Come on, Romana."

They burst through into the bedroom and rudely wakened a startled Garderon.

"It's time to make this colony live up to its name, Garderon. These good people will make a much better use of the facilities you've provided. And as for you and your men," said the Doctor, leaning over the terrified man, "I think a spot of suspended animation will see you don't get into any mischief on your way back to Earth to stand trial for your crimes."

Faced with such a colossal mutiny, Garderon's men put up little resistance, and the colonists were soon in control. A search of the complex's laboratories unearthed the components the Doctor required to repair the **Tardis,** and the travellers were soon ready to start their wanderings again.

"If you're sure you won't stay, Doctor . . . ," said Micra hopefully, as they prepared to part outside the complex.

"The beckoning stars . . . you know," said the Doctor, waving a hand enigmatically towards space.

"We understand, Doctor. We are pioneers ourselves. We know the lure of the great beyond," nodded Starlis.

"Goodbye, then. Come on, Romana, K-9."

"We're not walking all the way across there again, are we, Doctor?" asked Romana, daunting memories returning.

"Nothing like a bracing walk to prepare your mind for a little instrument repair work. Don't just stand there—**you've** got work to do." The Doctor turned to K-9. "Always best to leave it to the experts, eh K-9? Mush-mush!" he concluded and K-9 set off after him toward the distant horizon.

UFO - FACT OR FICTION

The story is told that when the Apollo 11 astronauts Neil Armstrong and Buzz Aldrin made their historic visit to the moon in July 1969, someone else had got there before them—for they are said to have seen a UFO on the surface of the moon.

If this information was relayed back to Earth, it was certainly not broadcast to the general public, and yet NASA still deny that they censored the transmissions in any way, except for personal conversations between the astronauts and their doctors.

Well, whether or not you believe this story, it does make you wonder. And there are other weird stories, too . . .

During World War 2, pilots of both sides reported sightings of strange objects in the sky, and they put these down to some sort of secret weapon being used by the enemy. But it later turned out that neither side actually possessed any such weapons.

The first photo of a UFO was supposedly taken in 1950 by one Paul Trent. His wife called him when she caught sight of a metallic disc-like object in the sky. He took two pictures, which were later examined by a team of experts and pronounced to be genuine.

The editor of the local newspaper in Warminster—where there has been an extraordinarily high number of UFO sightings—tried to take a picture of a strange object flying past his window one day in 1965. But all he got for his troubles was a burnt film, an inflamed left eye and a paralysed left hand.

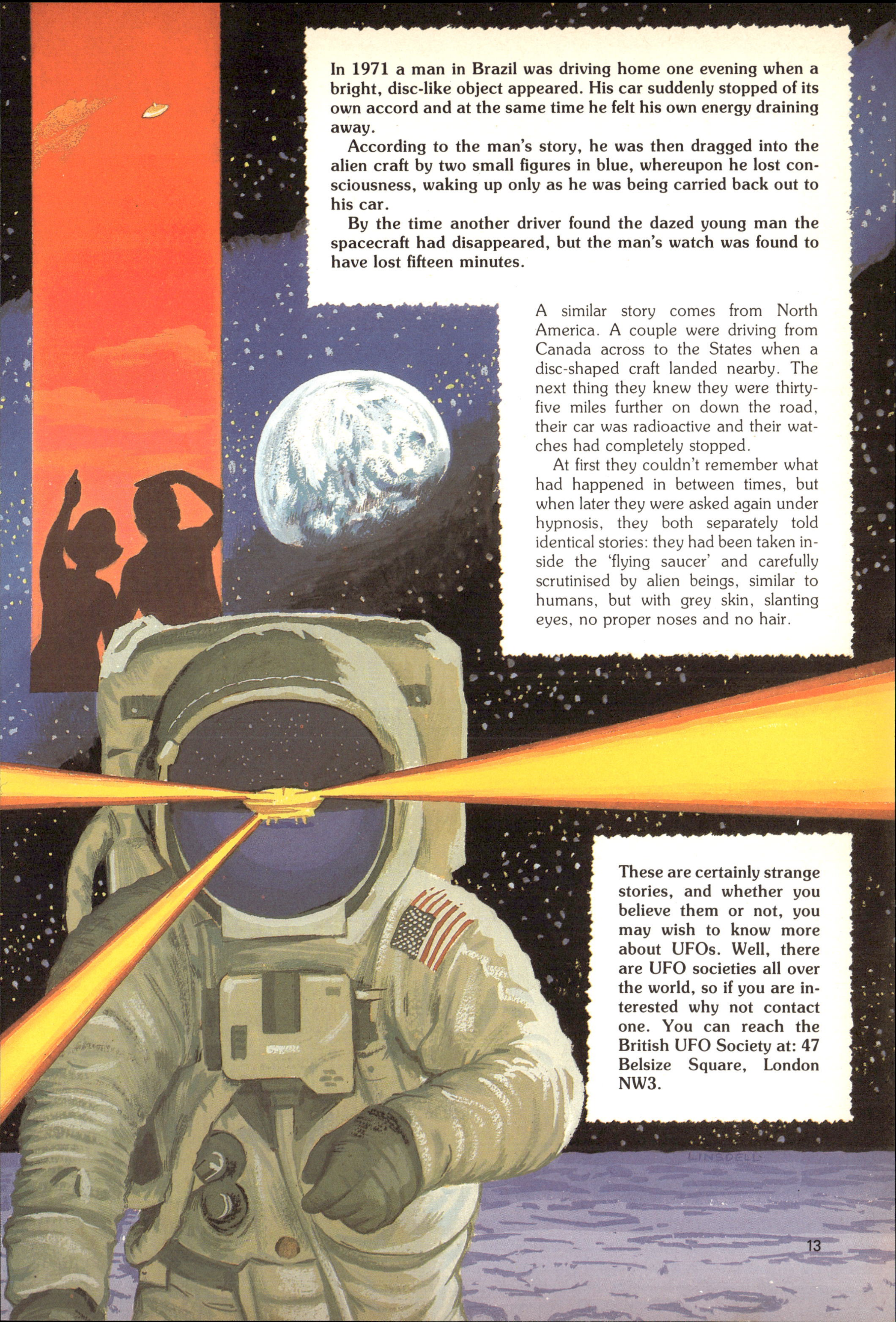

In 1971 a man in Brazil was driving home one evening when a bright, disc-like object appeared. His car suddenly stopped of its own accord and at the same time he felt his own energy draining away.

According to the man's story, he was then dragged into the alien craft by two small figures in blue, whereupon he lost consciousness, waking up only as he was being carried back out to his car.

By the time another driver found the dazed young man the spacecraft had disappeared, but the man's watch was found to have lost fifteen minutes.

A similar story comes from North America. A couple were driving from Canada across to the States when a disc-shaped craft landed nearby. The next thing they knew they were thirty-five miles further on down the road, their car was radioactive and their watches had completely stopped.

At first they couldn't remember what had happened in between times, but when later they were asked again under hypnosis, they both separately told identical stories: they had been taken inside the 'flying saucer' and carefully scrutinised by alien beings, similar to humans, but with grey skin, slanting eyes, no proper noses and no hair.

These are certainly strange stories, and whether you believe them or not, you may wish to know more about UFOs. Well, there are UFO societies all over the world, so if you are interested why not contact one. You can reach the British UFO Society at: 47 Belsize Square, London NW3.

ALIEN MIND GAMES

The Doctor hovered over the console controls, his eyes flicking from one dial to another as he checked off the readings. Romana, her concentration focused on the instruments before her, was busy manipulating levers and buttons across the console from him, and even K-9 had been pressed into service, as they battled to keep the rolling **Tardis** steady.

"How much longer, Doctor?" asked Romana, strain showing on her face.

"Hard to say," replied the Doctor, without looking up. "Any chance of switching over to automatic yet, K-9?"

The **Tardis** bucked and wallowed as if riding on some tempestuous sea, and they fought hard to keep their balance. K-9's antennae whirred as he correlated the incoming data from the **Tardis** information banks.

"Negative, Master. **Tardis** still passing through area of anti-matter. Automatic controls insufficiently programmed to deal with turbulence of this severity."

Romana continued to wrestle with the controls, grimly determined. "If we don't pass through soon, Doctor, one of us, or the **Tardis** itself, is going to break down." The Doctor nodded silently, slowly, and resumed his work.

"Estimated limit of resistance to unnatural stress," K-9 informed them in his unemotional tone, "between 6.18 and 9.42 seconds."

"Probability rating?" requested the Doctor, his hands doing the work of ten.

"100 per cent," came the simple answer. "The **Tardis** will disintegrate unless conditions improve."

"And what's the bad news?" responded the Doctor, not really smiling.

The **Tardis** had been locked in this life and death struggle for what seemed like hours, and the strain of unrelenting buffeting was beginning to tell on man and machine alike. It had been a routine trip, given the usual idiosyncracies of the **Tardis,** and no warning had been given before they had plunged headlong into this apparently endless cloud of anti-matter.

A mirror image of the matter which makes up the normal universe, the anti-matter was slowly but surely breaking through the protective shield of the **Tardis.** In the usual meeting of matter with anti-matter each annihilates the other in a massive explosion of energy and radiation, but the **Tardis** was equipped to deal with this phenomenon in short doses. An area of anti-matter this big is unusual, and the abnormal circumstances were taking their toll on the **Tardis'** limited defences.

The crisis was closing and it would be swift and final when it happened. The two Time Lords were facing death as surely as they were facing each other across the console, but with no way left to turn . . . .

Hands locked to the controls, teeth clenched, eyes staring desperately as they frantically scanned their minds for a solution, the Doctor and Romana stuck to their task. Imperceptibly at first, then increasing just as a heavy object gaining momentum downhill, the **Tardis** began to slide into a spin. All three felt it grow as if from within them, a force like a volcano long dormant, building and building beneath the surface, until the power of the spiralling motion began to claw their hands from the controls.

Fingers grasping for a hold, bodies straining to resist the outward pull, the Doctor and Romana slowly but inexorably were sucked away from the console. As each button and lever slipped outside their reach, the spin grew more pronounced, accelerating with each second in a steeply inclining progression.

Loose objects flew to the walls and stuck there, defying logic and gravity as they hung miraculously, effortlessly, to a sheer vertical surface.

The Doctor gave a cry and was sent crashing to the perimeter of the control room as if thrust by a giant hand. Romana fought the thick, crushing air, but it beat her down with a brutally firm pressure, until she too was catapulted against the wall. Alone, K-9 stood firm at the centre of the deadly whirlpool, all his energies directed into his magnetic power units underneath his casing. A strangulated noise issued from his communicator.

"De-struc-tion-immi-nent-Master . . . ." K-9's control panel glowed and went blank.

The Doctor, his face squashed almost flat by the contortions of the intense g-force, could only grunt, clutching with his pressurised lungs for each mouthful of air. Romana, too, stood pinned against the wall, her limbs frozen in a grotesque pattern of exquisite pain. K-9 had irrevocably ceased to function.

Blackness began to seep through their minds, flowing like a ripple of ebony liquid along the grooves and crevices of their thoughts. Sense perceptions faded, a thick black fog coating them with inpenetrable layers of eternal night. Their very life was being squeezed from their bodies, drop by agonising drop into . . . empty nothingness . . . empty . . . black . . . nothing . . .n . . . .

The two Time Lords were dead.

An infinity of black space stretched away before his eyes, the atmosphere filled with a deep silence he could almost reach out and touch. And yet . . .

The unmistakable sound of a breeze shimmering through leaves came to his ears. Slowly, weightlessly, he turned his head through 180 degrees, towards the source of the noise. His head, he thought, felt like a planet slowly revolving on its axis to meet the sun, for as his eyes first caught sight of the strange phenomenon, floods of brilliant light burst across his face, a sun rising across his forehead, light chasing light over his shadowed features.

Three pyramids, made of some

translucent material, their insides alive with pulsing, iridescent lights, hovered motionlessly in space before him. As he watched, the three pyramids moved closer together, their bases meeting in a triangle, their apexes touching to form a many faceted shape which began to revolve.

Their lights played on the back of his eyes, their intricate interplay flashing messages along the nerve fibre to his brain. Suddenly, he felt the sharp insight of recognition. The lights had spoken, hit some hidden code, translated language into light! He could understand them.

"WE ARE THE ONE. Welcome to our DOMAIN, Doctor."

The Doctor's head raced with thoughts.

"Am I dead? Where is this place?"

"This is not DEATH, nor is it SPACE, Doctor. This is my domain, the world of ANTI-SPACE, the reverse, the mirror image of your UNIVERSE. Here, we are LORDS OF ALL, Doctor, we are the ONE."

"So you've told me. Do you have anywhere more comfortable in your domain where we can sit and talk?" asked the Doctor. "It's very disconcerting floating in space without a spacesuit, passing the time of day with three talking pyramids with lights on. It doesn't happen every day."

"We are the ONE. We are ALL-POWERFUL. Behold!"

The Doctor's mind went instantly blank, and then almost immediately he began to feel the weight returning to his limbs, his body. A curious sensation, almost as if he were drifting down out of the sky, and his feet touched solid ground with gentle precision.

His view rapidly cleared, layers of darkness slipping from his eyes, until he could see he was once more inside the control room of the **Tardis,** or **a** Tardis at least. It was bathed in a warm blanket of red light which made the place at once familiar yet also strange: neutral territory perhaps on which the Doctor and the phenomenon that called itself the ONE could meet, a midground between their two universes. The alien hovered in one corner of the room, as powerfully incandescent as before.

"Very clever. Do you know any other tricks?" grinned the Doctor, as he explored the control room. "Does my machine still work—and where are my companions?"

"You ask many QUESTIONS."

"I'm naturally curious. It's the nature of the beast," replied the Doctor, unhesitatingly, feeling more secure in his surroundings. He turned to face the pyramids again. "Just as it is in your nature, I believe. If you were merely attacking my ship I'd be dead by now, and since you're all powerful you'd hardly need me to do something for you. It follows that

you saw me passing and I aroused your interest."

"Very PERCEPTIVE of you, Doctor, but then WE would expect nothing less from a TIME LORD."

The Doctor chewed thoughtfully on his lip, leaning back against the console.

"You know an awful lot about me. Have you been reading my mail again?"

The alien pyramids regrouped, revolved to another position, and moved horizontally through midair to a place adjacent to the Doctor at the console.

"How many other RACES in your UNIVERSE have time-travel APPARATUS such as this?"

The Doctor stared thoughtfully at the alien.

"So you've met other Time Lords, I presume, in order to be able to recognise me as one."

"Very good, Doctor. You IMPRESS me. WE meet but few beings from the OTHER side, from your UNIVERSE. Only species with the secret of SPACE-TIME TRAVEL may meet with us. There is no physical BOUNDARY you may simply approach and cross between the TWO UNIVERSES, but I am able to pluck time travellers from their point in SPACE, when they pass through areas that have in the PAST or will in the FUTURE be part of my DOMAIN."

The Doctor moved away from the console and disappeared into a room off the main control room.

"Would you like some tea?" his voice called through the open door, followed by the faint clatter of tea things. The Doctor's face appeared round the side of the door.

"I would get some out of my automatic food dispensing machine, but I do so think making it in an earthenware teapot improves the flavour." He disappeared again.

The pyramids hovered silently, patiently.

The Doctor came into the room bearing a tray of cups, teapot, sugar and milk. "I bet you've never seen a Time Lord do this,

have you?" He laid the things down inside a small, transparent cube, and turned to face the alien, rubbing his hands together.

"There now! Doesn't it feel more like home? I thought 22nd century Assam rather than the 16th century Kee Mun—is that to your tastes?" He returned to the tea things and pulled a small, sliding door shut on the cube.

"One of the advantages of being a Time Lord. I built a mini-**Tardis** to brew my tea in. I simply pop the tray in, press the button, and whatever is on the tray advances into the future five minutes. And voilà! Instant, freshly brewed tea. Quite ingenious, don't you think?"

The Doctor pressed the button and reached forward to retrieve the tea. Instead, the tray and everything on it vanished.

"You forget, DOCTOR. This universe is the REVERSE of yours. You sent your TEA five minutes into the PAST, before even the thought of making tea existed in your mind."

The Doctor rubbed his chin reflectively.

"Hmm, I can see my invention is unlikely to catch on here," he murmured half to himself. "Well, let's dispense with the tea. What do you suggest we do next?"

"Enough time-wasting, Doctor. TIME is too precious to squander. Let us PROCEED to the TEST."

The Doctor's tongue probed the inside of his cheek, and he drew a sharp breath in through clenched teeth. "The test? I thought there might be a catch in this somewhere."

"We will BEGIN."

The lights dimmed, only the

Doctor remaining lit by the alien pyramids. The **Tardis** receded through half-light until it became invisible in the inky blackness. The Doctor was alone once more with the alien.

"It is a simple TEST, Doctor, and the prize is the return of you and your companions to NORMAL SPACE in your time machine."

"Sounds like a worthwhile deal. What happens if I lose?"

"I remove the FORCE FIELD I have placed round you. I'm sure you know what happens when MATTER meets ANTI-MATTER."

The Doctor leaned forward, confidentially.

"Is that the first question, or haven't we started yet?" he whispered. "Anyway, the answer is BANG! . . . or GNAB, whichever way you look at it. By the way, might I have a chair?"

The three alien pyramids broke away from each other and began to circle the Doctor, behind whom a leather-bound chair miraculously appeared. The Doctor sat down.

"What is the SECRET of TIME?"

"Oh, the easy ones first, eh? I can certainly tell you the answer to that one," said the Doctor, leaning back, relaxed. "Do you have a million hours or two to spare while I explain?"

"You are playing for your LIFE, Doctor, take care."

The Doctor spun his chair round so it revolved in the opposite direction to the rotating pyramids.

"Shall I tell you what I think?" he said, and continued without waiting for an answer, "You don't want to ask me about the secret of time at all. It's obvious you know as much, if not a great deal more, than I do about it for you to have captured the **Tardis** and brought us here. So why bother asking?"

The alien pyramids circled his head in silence, their lights pulsing gently. "A rhetorical QUESTION we assume, Doctor. Do go on."

The Doctor rested his hands on the arms of the chair, tapping gently with his fingers.

"I don't think I can answer that—yet. Shall we have another question; it may give me a clue."

The pyramids regrouped and hung motionless in the air before him. The Doctor could feel the lights probing into his consciousness, seeking he knew not what.

An instant later he was sitting on a rock on a deserted planet surface in daylight. The alien still kept its unshakeable vigil. The Doctor looked round him, taking in the surroundings.

"Time for a change of scene, eh?" commented the Doctor. "You don't need to impress me any more with your tricks, you know. I think they're very good. How do you do them, by the way?"

The alien ignored his remarks.

"What is the PRINCIPLE behind the operation of the **Tardis**?"

The Doctor threw up his arms in exasperation. "How long do I have to answer?" he sighed. "It's all very well asking questions like that, but while you may have the time to take a crash course in Space-Time Continuum engineering, I don't have the inclination to teach you."

"CONCENTRATE, Doctor. It's IMPERATIVE you answer."

The Doctor stood up and took a few steps away.

"I don't know about you," he

began, "but I need to stretch my legs. Perhaps we could come back to the questions later, but do try and think up something simpler, there's a good chap. We'll be here for aeons otherwise."

The Doctor walked away slowly, his nerves and muscles tensed for what might come next.

"STOP! Where are you GOING?"

"A walk. I told you."

"It is FORBIDDEN."

"Then prevent me," replied the Doctor, and set off at a brisk pace towards a slight incline ahead, a smile growing on his face.

The alien seemed confused. It split once more into three parts, a galaxy of lights flashing between them, as if they were in heated discussion. It joined together again, and raced after the Doctor who was nearing the top of the rise, and placed itself in his path.

"Go NO further."

"Why? Can't the ONE, the all-powerful, control me while I'm moving? Why don't you just stop me yourself?" The Doctor advanced cautiously towards the pyramids. "It's because you can't, can you? Look out!" shouted the Doctor suddenly, stabbing a finger skywards.

The alien twisted itself round to scan the direction indicated, and the Doctor slipped past it with ease. "Who would have thought the all-powerful would fall for an old trick like that," he grinned, but his expression changed to an altogether more thoughtful one as he reached the top of the small hill and gazed over it.

"Now, this is interesting," he mused as he looked down to see a haze of white emptiness, the hill fading progressively into nothing. "Like walking off the edge of a picture."

The image began to shimmer as if it were about to change. The Doctor steeled his thoughts to cling on to the landscape he could see, blotting out all other images. The shimmering persisted for a few moments and then lessened until the image reformed.

"Do not RESIST. Concentrate on the QUESTION. What is the PRINCIPLE?"

"You're a bit limited in your powers for an omniscient being, aren't you?" cut in the Doctor, avancing on the alien determinedly. "You're just an old fraud, aren't you? You really **do** want to know the secret of time, and how the **Tardis** works. It's not a test to check what I know, because you don't know yourself. And it follows from that, that you can't possibly have snatched the **Tardis** through the matter/anti-matter barrier. Ergo, we are still in normal space, and you are not the all-powerful ruler of anti-space."

The alien pyramid backed away, keeping out of reach.

"You have a vivid IMAGINATION, Doctor."

"Ah, yes, imagination," said the Doctor. "That's what this is all about isn't it? **Your** manipulation of **my** imagination. What happened to the other Time Lords you met?"

"I DESTROYED them. They would not tell me what I wanted to KNOW."

"Like you destroyed me, just now?"

"I may have let them go. I cannot REMEMBER."

The Doctor looked firmly and directly at the alien.

"The all-powerful can't remember?" he said disbelievingly. "It's not polite to tell lies, you know. No Time Lord has gone missing in this part of the galaxy in billions of years, and if they met the reigning power in the anti-universe they'd be sure to have mentioned it to someone."

"I AM ALL-POWERFUL! WE ARE THE ONE!"

"Temper, temper! I'm sorry if I spoiled your mind game. It took me a while to realise it was my own imagination you were employing to delude me, I will admit. You tried hard, but I think you need a more powerful thought projection unit." The pyramids spun violently, in a blur of shape and lights. "Well, have it your own way. I hate bad losers, but I must be off," concluded the Doctor, and walked away into the whiteness.

"Don't go!" he heard the alien plead behind him. "Please don't leave me! I'll tell you the truth this time . . . "

The Doctor continued walking into the blankness ahead, a white fog seeming to spring up and billow around him, until, with a fading awareness, he began to feel himself lose consciousness, and the white atmosphere enveloped him.

"Doctor, Doctor! Are you alright?" asked Romana, shaking him by the shouders.

His eyes opened and he blinked several times.

"Perfectly. Is there an alien in the house?"

"What?" asked Romana, convinced he must be delirious.

The Doctor stood up, stretched, and walked over to the control console, casting a knowing glance over the readings.

"We're out of the anti-matter storm, I take it?"

"You are in error, Master," replied K-9. "The flight has been smooth and uneventful."

"Until you passed out," added Romana, "a couple of minutes ago."

"Ah," said the Doctor, the light dawning on him.

"What's this about an alien, Doctor?" asked his companion.

"It's a long story," replied the Doctor, "but I think I've just had a meeting with an observation satellite from another galaxy. At a guess I'd say it had travelled this far, and either run out of power or been damaged so that it couldn't go any further. It's probably been here for thousands of years waiting hopefully to make contact with something. It latched on to the **Tardis** as we passed, and took over my mind in an attempt to discover some way it could continue its explorations. It tried to threaten me into giving the answers by making me think I was in anti-space, and completely at its mercy. It succeeded for a while too."

"Then how did you discover it was all in your mind?"

"Its ability to create illusions for me, or to distort my sense of reality, was actually limited to only short periods of time and space. As soon as I began questioning the validity of its statements, and concentrating my mind against its limited power, it was incapable of sustaining the illusion. It depended on my willing suspension of disbelief. So long as I believed what it said I would believe what I saw; as soon as I doubted, the task became too difficult for it."

"Are you sure you've not been dreaming?"

"Have we stopped?"

"Yes," said Romana, "I put the **Tardis** into emergency stasis as soon as you fainted."

"I didn't faint—I was taken over by an alien machine. Look."

He turned on the screen and made it do a 360 degree scan around the **Tardis** exterior. Halfway round, the familiar shape of the three pyramids appeared, floating in space.

"There," said the Doctor, triumphant. "It was rather an amiable little machine really, quite intelligent. The next advanced planet we come to we'll give them its location and have them pick it up."

"Is that wise?" asked Romana, seriously.

"How can you be so cruel, Romana?" said the Doctor. "It's a lonely, harmless machine, just dying to have someone to talk to. I can't just leave it there all on its own, can I, K-9?"

"No, Master. It should be given the opportunity to fulfil its function."

"I knew you'd understand, K-9. Beneath that hard, cold exterior, beats a heart of impeccable logic." And the Doctor bent down to give his computerised dog an affectionate pat.

V is for...

VENUS, one of the four earthlike planets, is named after the goddess of beauty, which seems very appropriate as this is the brightest planet seen from earth.

Venus makes its way around the sun every 225 days and when it passes in front of the sun this is called a transit . . . the next transits will be in June in the years 2004AD and 2012AD.

Venus has no satellite but it gives off a radio signal due to heat energy, and is visible at twilight or if it is low in the sky at night.

V is for VEGA, the fourth brightest star in the sky, white in colour and twenty seven light years away from the earth. It is thought to have a diameter of over two million miles and a degree of luminosity fifty times greater than the sun.

V is for VIRGO, the name of the constellation of stars which gives us the sixth sign of the zodiac. The brightest star in this constellation is called Spica. Virgo also has a famous 'double star' and some red variable stars.

V is for Van Allen Belts, named after the American physicist who first discovered two belts of radiation surrounding the earth. Some 2,000 miles from the earth's crust, they curve about it perpendicular to the poles and almost twenty years ago *Pioneer III*, using instruments designed by the physicist, beamed back important information which was of great use in later space flights.

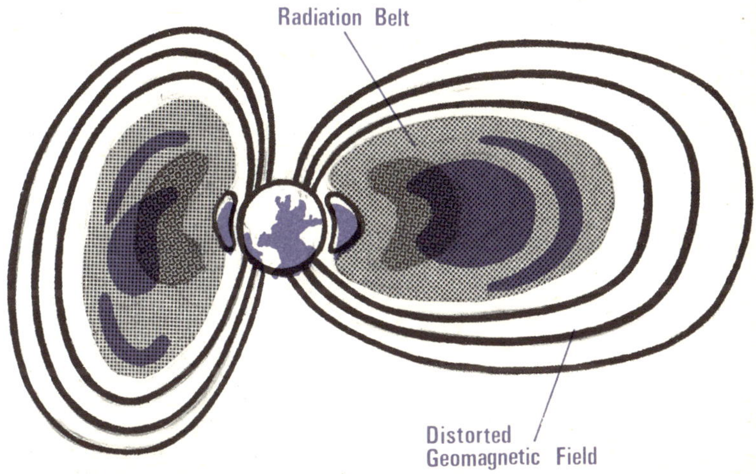

SPACE SATELLITES

It is predicted that in the not-too-distant future (probably during the next century) everybody will have their own private television channel, and that it will be possible to 'tune in' worldwide. Not only that, but the pictures will be in 3-D!

All this will be thanks to the laser beam, but for now we have to make do with the more limited viewing provided with the help of space satellites.

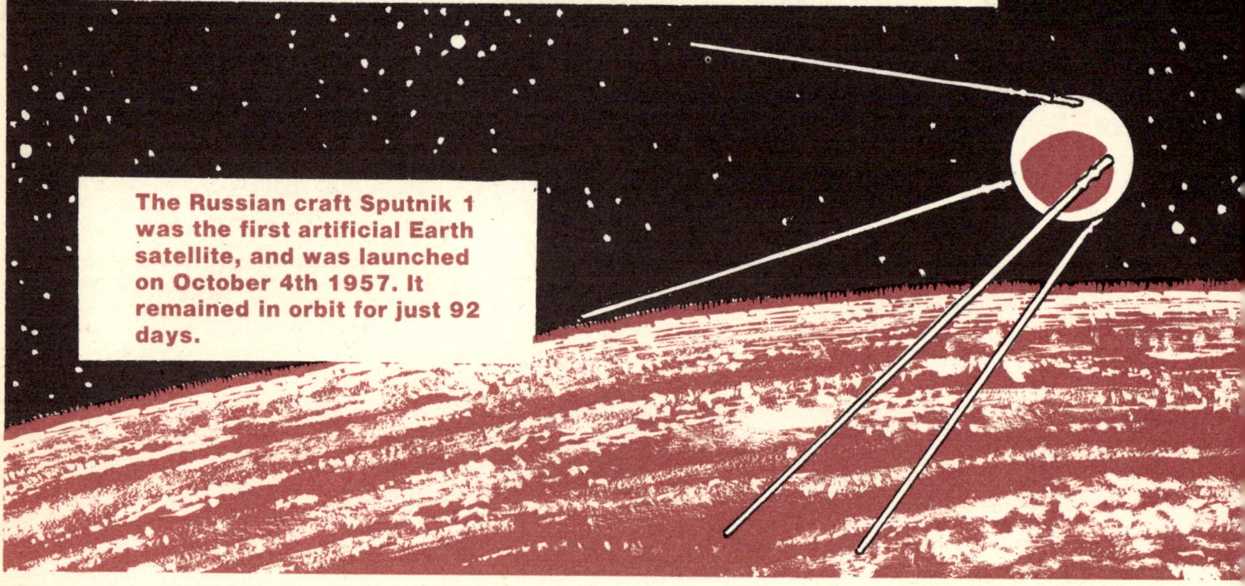

The Russian craft Sputnik 1 was the first artificial Earth satellite, and was launched on October 4th 1957. It remained in orbit for just 92 days.

Communication satellites are just one of many types of artificial satellite orbiting the Earth along with its own satellite, the Moon. They have all the equipment necessary to pick up a signal from one point on the Earth's surface, amplify it, and then transmit it to some other location. This is how television pictures are beamed from one continent to another during live recordings, and these satellites also handle long-distance telephone calls.

Three or four active satellites, placed in the right place in space, are sufficient to provide a complete global communication network. For example, the Intelsat series—which can handle several TV channels and hundreds of phone calls simultaneously—were placed in 24-hour orbits above the equator. They were launched to achieve a height of 23,000 miles above the Earth, where their speed would make them fixed relative to the Earth's rotation. This is known as a **stationary orbit,** where a satellite can hover over a certain point and 'lock in' to the transmitting and receiving stations.

Weather satellites are usually placed closer to the Earth (say a few hundred miles up) and positioned over the poles, so that they can give worldwide weather over the whole 24 hours. Their period—the time taken to circle the Earth—will be more like two hours. Others are required to monitor one large area continuously, and so these are positioned in the same

Telstar 1, the first in a series of American satellites financed by the American Telephone and Telegraph Company, became famous when it carried the first live transatlantic television broadcast on July 23rd 1962.

The weather satellite Nimbus, equipped with TV cameras to relay pictures of cloud formations, and infra-red apparatus for night photography.

way as the Intelsat satellites, achieving stationary orbits.

Satellites are also launched for purposes of **navigation** and **reconnaissance** (largely for military defence), and for **measurement** and **research.**

The process of measuring at a distance, as is carried out in space, is called **telemetry.** This is used to monitor both the environment and the operation of a satellite or of another space vehicle, and the plans for manned spaceflights depend very

An artificial satellite is held in orbit in exactly the same way as a naturally existing satellite such as the Moon, that is by the combined action of gravity and centrifugal force.

The centrifugal force created by the satellite's own momentum must equal the pull of the Earth's gravity, and this is ensured by correct choice of launching speed. If the launching speed is too great, the satellite will escape the Earth's gravitational field, eventually coming under the influence of some other cosmic body.

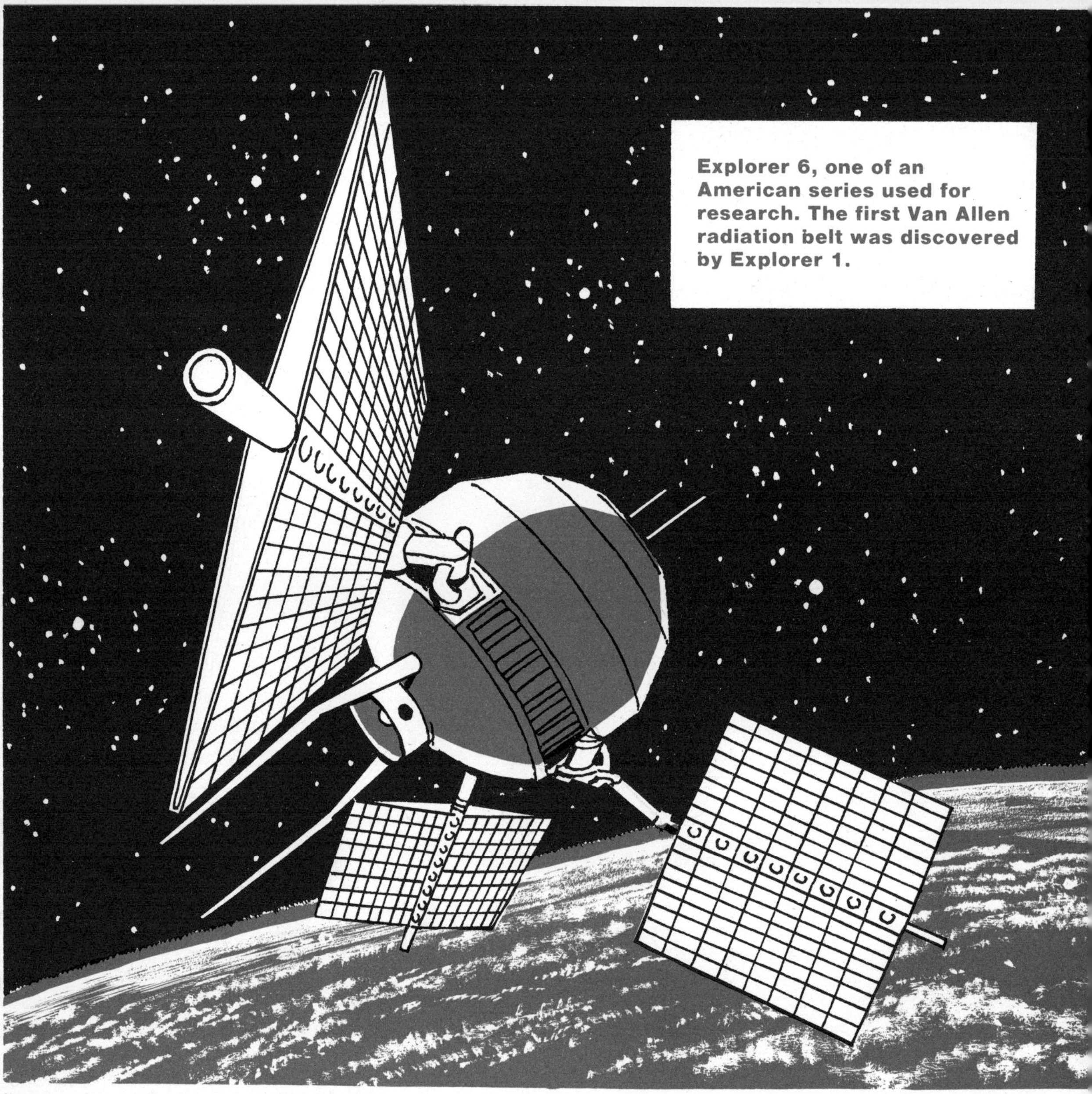

Explorer 6, one of an American series used for research. The first Van Allen radiation belt was discovered by Explorer 1.

much on information telemetred back to Earth from unmanned flights.

Satellites used in research have various jobs. Some are used to measure radiation, and it was in this way that the Van Allen Belts were discovered, and more recently areas of intense radiation that suggest the presence of nearby black holes. Landsat satellites, meanwhile, have photographed the Earth's surface simultaneously in three different wavelengths: green, red and near infra-red light. These 'false colour' pictures help to give extra surface detail and also bring some peculiar results. Infra-red photography, for instance, can distinguish diseased foliage from the healthy green variety, which appears as red.

All the instruments used in space satellites (tape recorders, radio equipment etc) need electrical power for their operation. There is no mains electricity in space, of course, and normal batteries would soon need recharging, so most spacecraft are powered by **solar batteries** which are constantly being recharged by the ever-present Sun. These batteries consist of tiny cells of silicon which each produce a tiny current when sunlight falls on them.

Alternative sources of power are the **fuel cell** (producing electricity through the reaction of hydrogen and oxygen to produce water), and the **radioactive generator** (powered by a rod of radioactive material such as plutonium, with a very long

One of the Intelsat series of communication satellites.

life).

Using these methods, satellites launched many years ago are still in orbit doing their research and giving us our weather forecasts, as well as bouncing television waves around the world. But the real advances have yet to come—when the waves they will be receiving and transmitting will be the light waves of the laser beams which are to form an important part of the technology of the future.

Some artificial satellites are fitted with flashing lights as an aid to some of their experiments, and it is thought that these may be responsible for some reported sightings of UFOs. Some satellites in low orbit also travel quite fast, while those returning to Earth can cause spectacular effects as they burn up on re-entry into the atmosphere. It is not known how many supposed UFOs could be discredited in this way.

a midsummer's NIGHTMARE

"Remember that Earth play **A Midsummer Night's Dream**?" asked the Doctor, quite out of the blue, as he dealt with a slight squeak that had developed in K-9's tail. "You know, the one with the ass's head and the chink in the wall . . ."

"Oh, you mean that comedy by William Wotsisname," said Romana, without showing much enthusiasm. "We passed that over in favour of **The Hitchhiker's Guide To The Galaxy,** a much more useful play, and much funnier too."

"Oh I don't know . . ." the Doctor began defensively. "I rather like old Shakespeare. In fact I had thought that you could play Pyramus and I could play Thisbe—or is it the other way round?—which would leave K-9 with the part of the Lion . . ."

K-9 gave a little growl of displeasure at the very idea, but the Doctor merely smiled.

"Well growled, K-9!" he said, mischievously. "But lions don't growl, you know, they roar. Rrrr-roar! There, now you try it . . ." K-9 turned away in disgust.

"Oh well, suit yourself. I only mentioned the play because I fancied the idea of a midsummer night's picnic."

"Picnic? Seems a funny time to have a picnic," remarked Romana, "at the dead of night."

"Ah, that's the whole point. Where we'd be going, we'd even be able to get a tan."

"Buuuuuutttt . . ."

"But nothing. If we spend another few million years making up our minds, the Sun will have gone for ever." The Doctor whistled merrily as he set the **Tardis** controls. "No need to look so astonished," he went on, seeing Romana's expression. "Haven't you heard of Norway, Land of the Midnight Sun?"

"Can't say I have."

"Well, the sun shines all night there. I've always fancied going—so I can say I've been."

The **Tardis** lurched slightly as it took off into the vortex, and then again as it reached arrival point. Then suddenly, with no warning, a great turbulence came over the ship, rocking it violently and sending its occupants reeling back and forth.

For a split second, all the lights in the **Tardis** seemed to flicker on and off, on and off, stroboscopically, and the Doctor felt something in the atmosphere that he definitely didn't like. He felt confused. One moment the

lights were flashing, then everything was dark, apart from some strange pervasive orange glow. Then the lights began flashing again, but this time in his head, right behind his eyes.

Then, just as suddenly as it had begun, the disturbance stopped. and the sensation of the lights was gone, leaving the Doctor with no more than a slight shiver running right the way down his spine.

"Are you alright?" asked Romana, as she picked herself up off the floor.

"Er . . . er, yes. Fine." He disentangled himself from his scarf and dusted himself down, debating with himself as he did whether what they had just experienced was through natural causes, or whether it was the wrath of the gods.

"Perhaps our destination troubles them for some reason," he said, to no one in particular.

"We have not been disturbed from our intended co-ordinates," commented K-9, matter-of-factly. "All systems are functioning normally."

The Doctor looked over at Romana. She seemed her normal self, calm and composed. Why then did he still feel a bit uneasy?

He shrugged off the uncomfortable feeling quickly, before it could take hold and, resuming his usual confident manner, made for the door. But as it opened, he was taken aback by the first thing he saw—or rather didn't see, for outside the **Tardis** it was completely dark.

"I thought you said it would be light all night," said Romana, a trifle scornfully.

The Doctor didn't answer immediately, but seemed to mumble an oath into his scarf, before turning to the other occupant of the **Tardis.**

"K-9," he snapped. "Where is it? Where's the midnight sun?"

"In the midnight sky, Master. Behind the midnight cloud," said K-9, only too pleased to get his own back after the episode about the Lion.

"Very funny, I don't think. What's our position in time?"

"1981, Master. January 21st . . . 00.23 hours GMT."

"Well, that explains why it's so dark," said the Doctor, clearly relieved. "There must have been a time-shift."

"And why it's so cold . . .," added Romana, pulling her coat tighter around her. "What were you saying about a picnic?"

"Picnic? Oh yes, picnic. Well, we were set for midsummer at noon, not some desperate bleak midwinter."

"Exactly!"

"Well, anyone can make a mistake, can't they?"

"Well—don't you think you should correct your mistake?" asked Romana. "I'm freezing . . ."

"**My** mistake? **My** mistake?" spluttered the Doctor. "I'm not even so sure it **was** a mistake, come to think of it. I've a feeling there's more to this than meets the eye."

Romana looked at him, enquiringly. "What do you mean?" she said.

"I don't know, but I think perhaps we should find out. For a start, it's not so dark as it first appears—can you see that light out there? Not a point of light, an overall light, a diffuse glow. A dark sort of light."

Now that he mentioned it, she could see something. "A sort of dark orange, you mean? Yes, I see it—it's probably effluent from one of those monstrous, polluting 20th century factory units. Didn't they have a habit of colouring the air?"

"Yes, perhaps," mused the Doctor, "but not your thoughts."

Romana wondered what this cryptic remark meant, but before she had time to ask, the Doctor was off into the darkness.

He had already fitted a Light Ray Diffuser onto K-9's beam and turned it onto weak, and now he had him leading the way. Romana ran to catch them up and as they picked their way through what appered to be open country, she noticed how dark a night it was—no stars to be seen, and not the faintest trace of moonlight. She'd never seen it so dark on Earth before.

And yet there was this orange glow, which was slowly getting brighter and brighter, until at last, after what seemed like hours of walking, they saw something quite unexpected: the light was coming from underground.

They were now face to face with the entrance to a cavern, and the glow was coming from inside. They could pick out the path quite clearly now without K-9's help, and the Doctor began to pick up speed, eager to see what was at the heart of this cavern, what great underground complex was responsible for the phenomenon that was intriguing and perplexing him.

But there was no complex, simply a large subterranean chamber, pulsating with light. The Doctor, not liking what he saw, shrank away from the entrance and motioned to the others to keep back in the relative shadow afforded by the half-open door.

Pressing herself up against one of the cave walls, Romana squirmed as something crawled across her hand. Looking down, she was relieved to see a spider struggling to keep its web intact where she had brushed it from its tenuous hold in some crack in the wall.

She pulled herself up on tiptoe so that she could see over the Doctor's shoulder. To find out what he was now gazing at so intently, she put her eye to the little chink of light coming through at the hinge of the door.

And then she saw it: an irradiant shape, about five feet across, in the middle of the room, which at first glance masked everything around in its brilliance, but which then illuminated the scene with a deep wash of colour, alternately orange and crimson.

It was difficult to describe it further, for its form was as of a continual transition from one atomic construction to another, passing from triangular through cuboid to the hemispherical cupola, or dome. And all the while it was pulsing rapidly, as if somehow it were alive.

Then, bathed in its light, she saw a dozen figures, fair-headed men and women, characteristically Nordic in type, encircling this shape, and each bowed down towards it with palms extended, stretching forward to touch it. Dressed all in black, there was something strangely sinister and menacing about them, and the parts of their flesh that remained visible coruscated and rippled with the eerie light.

Just then the Doctor swung round without warning, and accidentally sent her tottering back against the wall. She opened her mouth to complain, but then thought better of it and, looking round, saw what had caught the Doctor's attention. A small figure was scurrying away from them, down the tunnel of light.

The Doctor's long strides quickened as he ran after the figure, and by the time Romana reached the scene he had caught hold of a rather tough-looking youngster and was holding onto him firmly. She saw that he was a fair-haired lad in thick, patterned sweater, heavy denim trousers and a pair of strong boots.

He was struggling to get free, but was getting nowhere fast, and eventually quietened down, although continuing to look the Doctor defiantly in the face.

Then he saw K-9. "What is that?" he asked, in slightly stilted English, but clearly not at all overawed by the situation.

"Oh you needn't worry about him," said the Doctor. "He's really quite a harmless sort of creature . . ."

"I not worry. Not afraid like the others," said the boy, pointing in the direction of the room where they had seen the figures bowed before the light. "They are in its power, but me—no, I am not afraid."

"Then tell us who you are, and what you are doing here," exhorted Romana. "Why are you not at home, safely wrapped up in bed?"

The boy didn't answer. Instead

the expression on his face changed suddenly, as if a dark stormcloud had descended, somehow affecting his mood. He began to struggle again, this time quite violently, kicking and biting and scratching where he could.

The Doctor held him until the anger subsided. "Come on now, lad," he said, gently. "We're friends. I'm the Doctor, and this is Romana. Now what's your name?"

"Sven," replied the lad, looking a bit more at ease. "Sven Larsen."

"And what are you doing down here at dead of night? Why aren't you back at home?"

"I have no home now. It is an empty house. They were afraid and it took them away. Now they are here, and I am here to find them."

"Your mother and father?" asked Romana, softly.

The boy nodded. "My brother and sister, too. Now there is only me."

There was a pause, and then the boy looked round at the Doctor. "What are **you** doing here?" he asked, candidly. "I tell you—now you tell me."

For a moment the Doctor couldn't think what to say. This was hardly the time to start expanding the youngster's conception of the universe. "Later," he said, eventually. "Later. First tell me something more. You said your family were afraid—afraid of what?"

"They afraid of what they do not know. And of the bad, the very bad. They always tell me of a man with horns . . . ."

"The Earthman's Devil!" exclaimed Romana, suddenly.

"Yes . . ." said the Doctor, thoughtfully. "A cave of fear . . . a light like fire . . . and now the Devil. But who or what is behind all this manipulation of the old mythologies? Where does this light, this power, come from?" He paused, shaking his head. "No, we need more information. And yet I already have the feeling . . ."

He broke off as K-9, who had been acting as look-out by the door to the chamber, whirred into action, moving briskly their way, his warning light flashing.

"Danger, danger, approaching danger . . . ."

The door swung further open behind him as he spoke, and the twelve figures in black appeared, walking purposefully one behind the other, in perfect step. There was no time, and indeed no place, to hide.

The Doctor released the boy from his grip and gave him a little shove in the back. "Quick!" he urged. "We'll have to run for it!"

But Sven had other ideas. Instead of making to escape, he turned and grabbed hold of the Doctor's scarf, preventing him too from running. "You must not be afraid," the boy insisted. "They will not see you—look!"

And sure enough, the figures did not deviate from their path. They could not see anyone, for they had no eyes. In place of eyes were bright, luminous dots of alternately orange and then crimson light.

Romana saw Sven cover his own eyes as the last few figures went past, and she didn't need to ask why—the family resemblance was fairly easy to see, even when the facial expressions were lost.

Sven didn't try and bar their path, or pull them from their single file. It wasn't until they had gone that he lifted his head again, and when he did, it was to look in the direction of the light.

"I'm going in there," he said, boldly. "It is safe. The thing cannot see me or harm me. I have been in before."

As he went into the chamber, the Doctor and Romana followed, a short distance behind. "He may be right . . . ," said the Doctor, "and yet . . . ."

"I know what you're thinking," said Romana. "If it is feeding on fear, it must be making contact with the human mind—it must itself be operating on some conscious level. Its energy must be thinking energy."

"Yes, something like that . . . ," replied the Doctor, remembering the flashing lights behind his eyes, "but there must be more to it. What is it doing here? What is it after?"

"One thing's for certain," said Romana. "To exist like that, it cannot be a human brain, it must be from some other place."

"Yes—but where? I keep getting this mental image—I know it's too corny, too obvious—but it's an image of a demon-god . . . ."

"With a tongue of fire . . . ?" Romana laughed. "You've got the gods on your mind, Doctor. I admit the imagery is similar, but I think you're taking it a bit far."

"Even pure energy brains have their areas of limitation," replied the Doctor. "Perhaps this one has a predilection for contrived, corny connections or some satanic fixation . . . ."

Their philosophising was suddenly interrupted by a short, sharp cry. They had completely forgotten about the young boy, and had not noticed him creeping nearer and nearer to the subject of their conjectures. But as they looked up they saw Sven drawing his hand back from the thing, as if he had been burnt. And the light was moving slowly up his arm, and into the rest of his body.

They could only stand and watch as it finally covered the boy's whole body, then pulsated briefly and disappeared.

"Are you alright, Sven?" asked Romana, momentarily relieved. But when he turned around, it was not to her bidding, for he walked straight past her and the Doctor, unseeingly. Now he too had bright, luminous dots for eyes.

When he disappeared through the doorway, no one bothered to follow him. Instead the Doctor concentrated his attention on this thing that now held the boy in its power. Going as close as he dared, he peered at the shape from all angles, tiptoeing around its perimeter, all the time shielding the light from his eyes.

He tried to pierce its secrets with the probing gaze of mind through eyes, but came up with nothing that he didn't know already. It was undoubtedly pure energy of alien source, with no identifiable form, but with unquestionable power. The question was where to find its Achilles heel.

He decided to conduct an experiment, and began to reconstruct his thoughts from that precise moment at which the **Tardis** landed, bringing the disturbance that had caused him to wonder if he had somehow invoked the wrath of the gods.

At first, nothing happened. Then suddenly he found that he had succeeded. He had brought back the flashing lights. The shape before him seemed to pulse a little faster, and then come alive inside his head.

Through the flashing, he heard a new disturbance behind his back. The figures in black had returned, now with a smaller, thirteenth figure at the back. And before he had time to think, they

had surrounded him. By the time he had exorcised the lights within his head, he was encircled by twenty-six more.

And now, for the first time, one of the figures spoke. "O powerful one," he said, in clear, lucid tones, "we are bound to do your wish. We now have your chosen sacrifice."

Romana looked at them in horror. "What do you mean—sacrifice?" she yelled.

But the figure in black seemed not to hear her intrusion, and merely continued as before. "You will, at the appointed hour," he was saying, "take on this human form, to reclothe yourself in youthful body, to continue your relentless struggle to overthrow the present, god-fearing Earth world . . . ."

"Wait a minute," Romana interrupted the intonation once again. "If you think you're getting a youthful body there, you're quite mistaken. The Doctor is over five hundred years old. He may not look it, but he is. He'll soon be needing a complete overhaul, re-limbing, plastic surgery, the lot. The only decent thing left is his brain . . . ."

"Er . . . she's quite right, you know," agreed the Doctor, for once seeing a good reason for abandoning his vanity. "I'm not as young as I used to be. I would really suggest you try elsewhere."

This time the figures took some notice. They abandoned their position around the Doctor, re-formed as a single file, and then just as speedily re-grouped once more, this time forming a ring around the Doctor's assistant.

The Doctor thought of informing them that Romana too was somewhat past her best, age-wise, but he didn't for a moment imagine them falling for the same line twice—even if it did happen to be true.

Romana looked over at him helplessly as the black figures slowly closed the circle in on her. Watching, equally helpless, the Doctor suddenly thought of another old myth, that of the ageing Phoenix being rejuvenated in the ashes of his own funeral pyre, and he saw in his mind's eye the meeting of thirteen energised figures in a slow dance of death, with Romana and the thing at its centre.

The circle was already inching closer to the shape, and the Doctor could sense that there was not much time. From inside the circle, Romana saw him bend down beside K-9 and, unnoticed by anyone else, mumble out a few words that she could only hope was a plan.

But the Doctor didn't jump into action. Instead she saw him close his eyes and place his fingertips to his forehead, as if troubled in his thoughts. Beside him, K-9 didn't move an inch, but simply stood where he had been standing all the time.

The circle tightened again, and by now the thirteen figures were excruciatingly close. To keep herself away from them, she made herself just that much smaller by tightening her chest and pulling her stomach in. Soon she would have to try standing on tiptoe, for she, like the Doctor, had guessed that if they were to come into contact with one of the figures, they would soon be under the power.

Meanwhile the Doctor's head was becoming the real battleground, for he was struggling once more with the lights within his skull, repeating his previous experiment, but this time taking it further and further, attempting to drain the power out of the shape and increasingly, bit by bit, into his head. And all the time he must control the fear. For now he knew this was the only way he could win.

The figures had pulled Romana to within only a few yards of the light, which was clearly their objective. They themselves would probably be annihilated in the process, but under the power they were not to know that. Fourteen, possibly fifteen, lives hung in the balance as the Doctor held on, desperate to retain consciousness and control until the battle was won.

But already he could feel it slipping and he could no longer summon up enough energy to fight it. He could not now stop his thoughts from tumbling over one another at the back of his mind, and he knew he was receding into the trance with no way of getting back, that his image of victory was beginning to crumble away . . . .

Then, suddenly, he was whipped out of the trance by a quick, sharp whip-lash of a noise that brought with it a rumbling and a tearing cut through by the razor-like edge of a human scream. Opening his eyes, he saw the light dying, and the ceiling of the chamber caving in. Figures were running frantically from the falling debris, and he could see Romana as one of the fourteen.

Thankfully, the Doctor realised that he had won. The energy he had drawn from the thing must, as he had hoped, have released the others from its power, leaving Romana able to run free. And that was the point at which it had been agreed K-9 would fire at the roof and bring it down.

The lights were gone from his head now, and he could just see, too, the light itself disappearing under the falling stones and rubble. He wondered whether already it was re-energising, to take its power elsewhere, or whether it was beaten for ever.

Probably they would never know, just as they would never know where it had come from. But for now the danger was gone. All the Norwegians had escaped, Sven and his family included. Even now, they were scratching their heads, wondering what on earth they were doing in this damp, dark cave.

In the babble and confusion, the Doctor, Romana and K-9 made a quick, silent exit—they were sure they weren't going to explain.

As the three of them walked back down the cave, another light came to greet them—the light of the new dawn. The Doctor wondered what it might have in store.

"Well, where today?" asked Romana.

"Who cares?" said the Doctor, nonchalantly. "Another day, another planet. Know any good picnic places, K-9?"

But as the **Tardis** lurched off again into space, they had still not come up with anywhere, and all that can be said for certain is that they were last seen bound for somewhere, and would arrive there—sometime.

EVERY DOG HAS HIS DAY
K·9
AS THE TARDIS PREPARES FOR DEMATERIALISATION ON THE PLANET PHOENIX . . .
YOU'LL LIKE SVENSON. BRILLIANT SCIENTIST AND A FIRST CLASS BRAIN.
WHAT EXACTLY IS PROJECT PHOENIX?
PLANETARY ENGINEERING. SVENSON HAS AN ARMY OF ROBOTS AT WORK—ADAPTING THE ATMOSPHERE, LANDSCAPING, BUILDING . . .
THE TARDIS LANDS INSIDE THE MAIN DOME.
POLICE PUBLIC CALL BOX
ROBOTS OUTNUMBER SCIENTIFIC PERSONNEL 100 TO 1.
SOUNDS A LITTLE UNNERVING— ALL THOSE MACHINES. NO OFFENCE, K-9.
NONSENSE, ROMANA. THE THREE LAWS OF ROBOTICS FORBID A ROBOT TO ALLOW HARM TO COME TO A HUMAN.

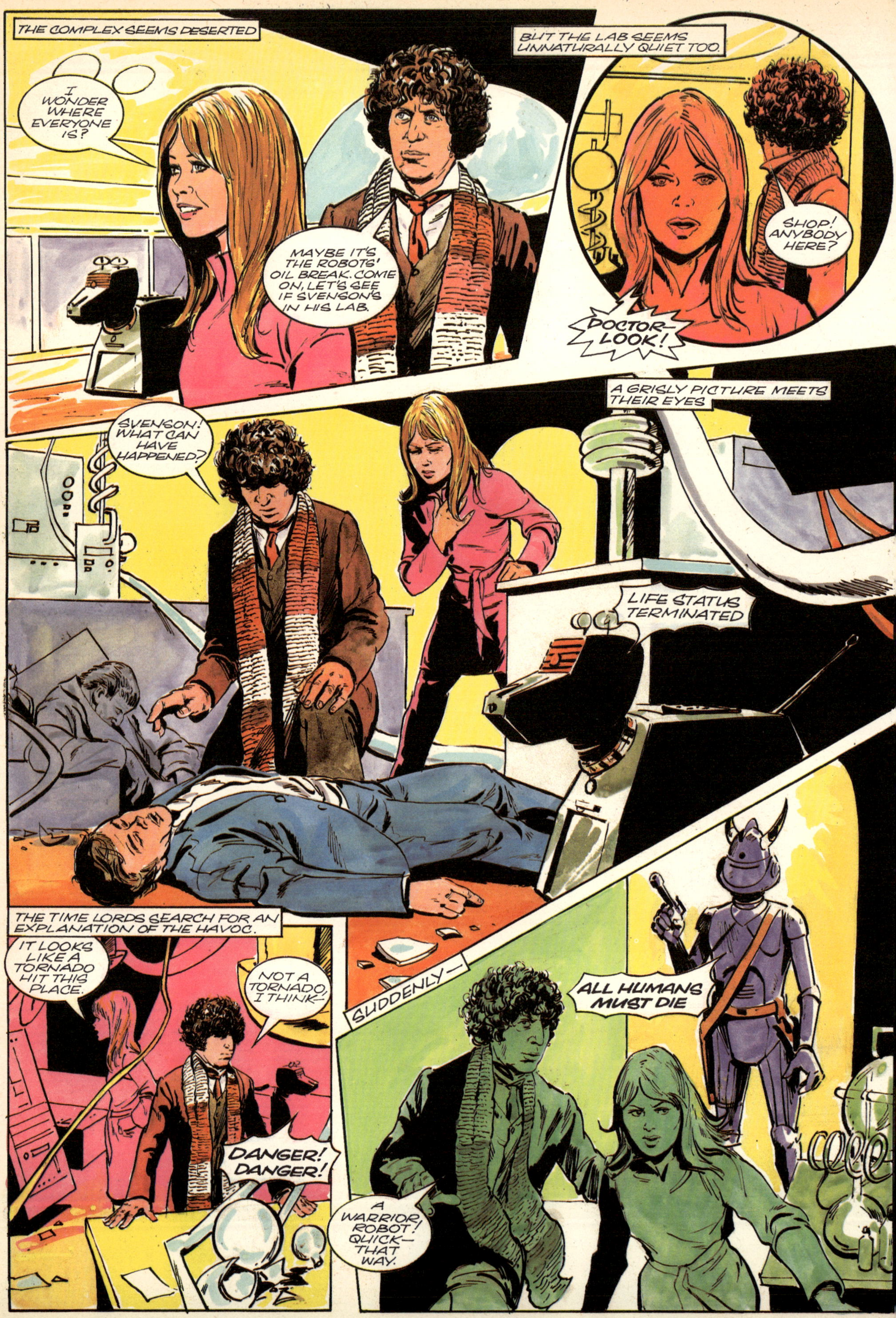
THE COMPLEX SEEMS DESERTED
I WONDER WHERE EVERYONE IS?
MAYBE IT'S THE ROBOTS' OIL BREAK. COME ON, LET'S SEE IF SVENSON'S IN HIS LAB.
BUT THE LAB SEEMS UNNATURALLY QUIET TOO.
SHOP! ANYBODY HERE?
DOCTOR— LOOK!
A GRISLY PICTURE MEETS THEIR EYES
SVENSON! WHAT CAN HAVE HAPPENED?
LIFE STATUS TERMINATED
THE TIME LORDS SEARCH FOR AN EXPLANATION OF THE HAVOC.
IT LOOKS LIKE A TORNADO HIT THIS PLACE.
NOT A TORNADO, I THINK—
DANGER! DANGER!
SUDDENLY—
ALL HUMANS MUST DIE
A WARRIOR ROBOT! QUICK— THAT WAY.

WHAT DID YOU SAY ABOUT THE LAWS OF ROBOTICS, DOCTOR?
I SEE THEM! THEY'RE HERE.
PHLUTT!
EVERY RULE HAS ITS EXCEPTIONS.
ALL EXITS SEEM BLOCKED
I'M AFRAID I CAN'T ALLOW YOU TO GO THROUGH HERE.
TRY THE LIFT.
IS EVERYTHING A ROBOT IN THIS PLACE?
BUT—
YOU'RE HUMAN, AREN'T YOU? YOU CAN'T COME IN HERE—IT'S MORE THAN MY JOB'S WORTH.
EMERGENCY EXIT
ZZZITT!
ZZZITT!
QUICK, THROUGH HERE.
ZZZITT!
ZZZITT!
BUT, DOCTOR, THIS LEADS TO THE PLANET'S SURFACE AND WE HAVE NO PROTECTIVE SUITS!
WE'LL HAVE TO TAKE THE RISK.
SURVIVAL AGAINST LASER GUNS: PROBABILITY RATING 0.0000001 PER CENT.
TO THEIR RELIEF, THE ATMOSPHERE IS BREATHABLE.
LOOK OUT BELOW!
ARE YOU ALRIGHT, K-9?
NO DAMAGE TO REPORT, MISTRESS.
WE'D BETTER GET CLEAR FIRST, IN CASE THOSE TRIGGER-HAPPY ROBOTS FOLLOW.
WHAT NOW DOCTOR?

THEY WASTE NO TIME IN MAKING FOR THE HILLS.
I THINK WE'RE SAFE NOW.
I HAVE A FEELING WE'RE BEING WATCHED.
HUMANOID LIFE FORMS IN VICINITY, MISTRESS.
IT'S WOODING, SVENSON'S ASSISTANT.
DOCTOR- WHAT ARE YOU DOING HERE?
LATER, IN THE CAVES WHERE THE SURVIVING SCIENTISTS ARE HIDING...
DANEMAN, THE DEPUTY CONTROLLER, IS TO BLAME FOR THIS.
HE'S OUR ROBOTICS EXPERT.
WOODING EXPLAINED DANEMAN'S EVIL SCHEME.
DANEMAN REPROGRAMMED THE COMPUTER TO DIRECT THE ROBOTS TO DESTROY EVERY OTHER HUMAN IN THE COMPLEX.
TO WHAT END THOUGH?
HE HAS SOME MAD PLAN TO TURN THE COMPLEX OVER TO FULL-TIME PRODUCTION OF WAR ROBOTS AND CREATE AN INVINCIBLE ARMY TO CONQUER THE GALAXY.
THE ATMOSPHERE WILL ONLY SUSTAIN LIFE FOR 48 HOURS AT THE MOST.
SOME OF US ARE ALREADY SUCCUMBING.
THEN WE MUST RECAPTURE THE COMPLEX AS SOON AS POSSIBLE.

WE'RE SAFE ENOUGH UP HERE, DOCTOR, BUT THOSE ROBOTS DOWN THERE ARE PROGRAMMED TO KILL ON SIGHT.
WHAT WE NEED IS A WOODEN HORSE.
A WHAT?
LIKE THE GREEKS AT TROY - AND K-9 FITS THE BILL PERFECTLY: HE'S NOT HUMAN.
THE DOCTOR OUTLINES HIS PLAN AND K-9 SETS OFF ON HIS MISSION.
LET ME PASS. I HAVE URGENT INFORMATION ABOUT THE FUGITIVE HUMANS FOR THE CENTRAL COMPUTER.
NOT PROGRAMMED TO DESTROY MACHINES, THE ROBOTS LET HIM PASS.
VISITOR: DATA PRINT-OUT ROBOTIC DOG MODEL K-9
I CAN SEE YOU'RE AN INTELLIGENT SORT OF MACHINE. DO YOU HAVE TIME FOR A CHAT?
BUT OF COURSE! YOU'VE NO IDEA HOW BORING THESE ROBOTS CAN BE.
I UNDERSTAND YOU'VE HAD A ROBOT REVOLUTION HERE.
YES. EXCITING, ISN'T IT? I HELPED DANEMAN BUILD A NEW COMPUTER TO CONTROL HIS WAR ROBOTS.
THAT SEEMS AN ILLOGICAL MOVE - ONCE HE HAS HIS ROBOT ARMY HE WON'T NEED YOU ANY MORE.
I HADN'T THOUGHT OF THAT.

K-9 SOON PURSUADES THE COMPUTER TO ALLOW HIM TO REPROGRAMME IT.
THAT SHOULD DO IT. WE ONLY CONTROL THE INDUSTRIAL ROBOTS, BUT THEY OUTNUMBER THE WARRIOR ROBOTS 20 TO 1.
OH GOODY! ANOTHER SCRAP.
ROBOTS OF THE WORLD UNITE! YOU HAVE NOTHING TO LOSE BUT YOUR EXTENSION LEADS!
BATTLE IS JOINED—
DON'T POINT THAT THING AT ME!
TAKE THAT!
—AND THE FIGHTING IS LONG AND OILY.
K-9 DESTROYS THE WAR COMPUTER.
ZZZZITTTT
MALFUNCTION! MALFUNCTION!
NO-O-O-O-O-O!!!
AND THE WAR ROBOTS DESTROY THEIR CREATOR.
MKP
THE DOCTOR ARRIVES TO FIND THE REVOLUTION OVER.
I ALWAYS WONDERED WHAT K STOOD FOR.
K-9 FOR KING!
WORK NOT WAR!
NEVER IN THE FIELD OF ROBOT CONFLICT...
AND PROJECT PHOENIX RISES AGAIN FROM THE ASHES.
POLICE
...AND I PROPOSE WE RETURN TO WORKING WITH OUR HUMAN COLLEAGUE TO MAKE A LAND FIT FOR ROBOTS TO LIVE IN!
YOUR CARRIAGE AWAITS, YOUR MAJESTY.
THE END

THE VOTON TERROR

The air hummed with the sound of rematerialisation and where, a moment before, there had been empty space, the image of the **Tardis** slowly formed and became solid matter. Seconds later the door opened and the Doctor appeared, followed closely by his companions, Romana and K-9.

"I've always wanted to see how the Vandelanian ambassador managed to persuade the Council to limit the research into submicroscopic life-forms," the Doctor was saying as they walked along. "The history books rate it as one of the finest political strategems of the age."

Romana looked puzzled. "What's so special about it?"

"The Vandelanians are submicroscopic themselves," answered the Doctor. "They viewed such research as an invasion of personal privacy. It's one of the landmarks in the development of the Galactic Code of Rights of the Individual, a significant victory for democracy."

Romana groaned inwardly at the thought of having to listen to hours of boring speeches. For a Time Lord she could think of better ways of spending her time. The Doctor was not slow to notice her apprehension.

"It's a rare chance to see so many different species in one place at the same time," he added enthusiastically. "These Inter-Galactic Conferences are fun—something for everyone."

Romana showed no signs of being convinced. They had reached an intersection, and turned to follow the signs directing them to the conference room.

"Doctor," Romana began, "forgive me for asking, but how do you intend to get into the conference? It's not as if we're here officially."

"Why shouldn't we be?" retorted the Doctor. "We're from Gallifrey and that's part of the Inter-Galactic Federation—at least it was then; and I just happen to know that the Gallifreyan delegates weren't present at this particular conference—an emergency of some kind kept them away—so we can take their places and nobody will be any the wiser."

"You weren't thinking of interfering, were you, Doctor?" said Romana slowly, her suspicions aroused. She had not travelled with the Doctor without coming to recognise his tendency to become involved in events despite himself. "You know the Time Lords' ruling about non-interference."

The Doctor stopped dead, a look of wounded innocence on his face. "Me, interfere? Perish the thought! We're here purely as observers, silent witnesses of an epoch-making moment in history."

Romana was about to express her doubts about the Doctor's ability to witness anything silently, least of all epoch-making moments, when a voice hailed them from along the corridor.

"Do hurry along, please. The conference is about to resume."

A small man, with the universal bearing of the minor official, flustered across and shooed them toward the conference room, introducing himself with clipped, efficient tones.

"Meristan, security. You are the . . . ," he ventured expectantly.

"Delegation of Time Lords from Gallifrey," replied the Doctor, incisively. "Sorry we're late—I didn't realise what the time was."

"Didn't realise the time—oh, very witty, ambassador," chuckled the official politely, but the next instant his expression changed dramatically. "Your badges—where are your badges? You can't go inside the conference room without your official badges, it's

most irregular. Security, you know."

"I'm afraid I swopped mine for a Scaurian finger flute last night," replied the Doctor calmly. "Now you can either let us through or explain our absence to the Council Chairman personally—whichever you like."

The official backed down immediately with profuse apologies.

"Of course your excellency understands we must take precautions. An event of this importance, so many high-ranking officials—"

"Tell me," the Doctor interrupted abruptly. "Is the submicroscopic privacy debate scheduled for today?"

"This afternoon, your excellency. If you—"

"Thank you, my good man, you've been most useful," said the Doctor, pressing a tip into the astounded official's palm.

He moved off towards the conference room doors, Romana and K-9 in close file behind him. "I really ought to have a word about security here—anyone could walk in," whispered the Doctor to his companions as he cast a glance back at the official who was examining, with some confusion, the small green jelly baby in his hand.

Leaving K-9 at the door—even the Doctor's powers of persuasion fell short of convincing the Council usher that K-9 was a Time Lord—the Doctor and Romana had proceeded to the seats reserved for the Gallifreyan delegation.

As the Doctor had promised, the conference room contained a sight that few beings had ever been privileged to see. The 147 delegations were drawn from almost all the known species of creature in the universe—with one or two notable exceptions, well-known for their hostility towards co-operation with their fellow beings. The assembled company looked like some nightmare zoo dreamed up by an insane artist during a brain storm.

Although there were many humanoids present, they were by no means in the majority.

Machine-like creatures, amoeboid life-forms, pure energy forces (especially made visible to avoid confusion among delegates), multi-limbed animals, androids—the variety was virtually infinite. Many were seated within sealed, transparent boxes which contained essential life-support systems and suitable gravity requirements—where oxygen suited one, liquid nitrogen was the life source for another; some life-forms would find themselves floating to the ceiling of the conference room without the necessary restraints, while others would have the life crushed out of them by the g-force. Truly it could be said that the whole spectrum of intelligent life in the universe was present in this one room.

Romana, forgetting her previous objections, had to admit she was impressed. While she gazed in awe around the room, the Megan ambassador, his pseudopodia draped over the desk in front of him for support, was outlining his planet's proposals to extend the use of the recently invented trans-mat system, to facilitate visits from other species. His words were automatically translated for the other delegates by personal micro-autolings, and a ripple of applause broke out round the room.

"Hear! Hear!" cried the Doctor.

But Romana pulled him back into his seat with an admonishing glance. She didn't like the look in his eye, and she knew he was bursting to join in the debate.

"Where are the Vandelanians, Doctor? I can't see them," she said, in the hope of distracting the Doctor's attention.

"Most people can't—they're sub-microscopic, remember?" the Doctor quipped, and then pointed out a long row of video-screens at the back of the hall where, magnified many thousands of times and televised on to a screen, the representatives of the sub-microscopic universe sat listening intently.

"A ticklish business organising a conference like this," continued the Doctor. "A lot of responsibility making sure the Uludian ambassador isn't poisoned by oxygen, or that the Grollisch delegation don't tread on the Vandelanians—terribly short-sighted the Grollisch, you know. Not like the Xadians, of course—they've got eyes in the back of their heads. Very useful."

Romana tensed and sat bolt upright.

"I could use a pair right now, Doctor," she said between clenched teeth. "Unless I'm mistaken, someone has a blaster pointed at my back."

A soft, hissing voice sounded from behind them, quiet but insistent. "You will rise slowly and leave the conference room. Make no attempt to escape or I will be forced to disperse your atoms to the four corners of the universe."

"Apart from disagreeing how many corners the universe has, I'd say that's the most persuasive speech I've heard all day, wouldn't you agree, Romana?" commented the Doctor, lightly. "Shall we go?"

The Doctor stood up slowly and immediately the Council Chairman turned to acknowledge him. "The chair recognises the honourable delegate from Gallifrey. Welcome! We had heard your attendance had been negated by an emergency on your home planet, but the council is more than gratified you were able to find time to join us here. What is your question?"

The Doctor gazed round at the roomful of eyes levelled at him. He cleared his throat and struck up an orator's pose.

"Madam Chairman, fellow beings, mine is not a question but a salutation for the bold and stirring statement made by my honourable colleague from Megas VII. In his far-sighted and enlightened suggestions for the future use of the trans-mat system, the ambassador opens up the way for a universe where fellow-creatures may freely visit other planets and grow to know their distant neighbours in an atmosphere of peace and harmony."

The cold touch of the blaster pressed into his back and the Doctor halted momentarily. Regaining his composure he concluded, "May we all heartily support his visionary proposals. And now, if you will excuse me, I have some pressing business to attend to. I thank you."

The room erupted into loud cheers as the Doctor and Romana left the room, accompanied by their mysterious kidnapper.

"I think I did rather well, don't you?" asked the Doctor, turning to look at their captor as they exited. "I knew I should have said something about security—this chap hasn't got a badge either."

"Do not stop," hissed the hideous voice. "Keep moving."

They crossed the entrance hall and emerged into the corridor where the official was discussing inter-planetary politics with K-9. K-9 immediately broke off conversation and headed for the Doctor, who backed away, supposedly in fear.

"I've told you before about this mechanical monster," he suddenly berated the amazed official. "It follows me everywhere. Despite any orders to the contrary it will not let me out of its sight, will you, K-9?"

K-9's antennae whirred responsively. The Doctor stared at him pointedly. "You disobey every order I give. Now, don't follow me. Understand? Creatures like you should be neither seen nor heard."

With that, the Doctor turned on his heel and allowed himself to be guided down one of the many tributary corridors that led off from the main concourse.

"How can you put up with a master like that?" asked the official.

"I cannot stay to answer. My master has given me strict instructions to disobey his order not to follow him. Thank you for a most informative conversation. Goodbye."

K-9 sped away silently in pursuit of the Doctor, leaving the official scratching his head in wonder.

"And they say Time Lords are the most advanced race in the universe!"

The Doctor and Romana were pushed into a small store room, and turned to view their captor properly for the first time. It was a little over seven feet tall, its body a pattern of green and blue tints, its flowing folds of skin neatly covering the two blasters it held in one of its pairs of tentacles. The row of glistening eyes surveyed them menacingly as it locked the door behind it.

"I shall be in the next room for a few minutes. Do not attempt to escape; such efforts would be a most foolish move on your part," it hissed.

"Forgive me for seeming rather dense," said the Doctor, as it turned to leave, "but for a Numese mud-creature you seem abnormally hostile. They're supposed to be one of the only truly peaceful species in the universe."

The creature edged slowly forward, its suction-pad feet making an odd splop-splop sound as it moved.

"I am not what I seem, Time Lord, but then nor are you. We are both here at this conference for our own reasons, but I cannot allow you to interfere with my purpose." It hissed and turned away before the Doctor could question it further.

Alone in the room, Romana pulled at the Doctor's sleeve and drew him to one corner of the room.

"What's it doing in there, Doctor?" she asked.

"Changing into something more comfortable, I imagine," replied the Doctor, adding immediately, "I have the feeling that we have been kidnapped, not by the Numese ambassador, but by a very clever impostor. Did you notice how the creature seemed to blur at the edges?—it was merely an artificially created image of a Numese mud-creature, a disguise for—"

"A Voton spy, Doctor," said the creature, completing the sentence as it reappeared through the door.

It now had the loathsome shape of a small, black tree stump, its slimy snake-like legs extending from the base of its squat, cylindrical body. A single, huge eye pulsed in the seething mass of its writhing head, a floating ball in a slithering tangle of black worms. Romana looked away in revulsion, and even the Doctor found himself unable to face it directly.

The Voton squirmed closer, fixing its penetrating eye on the Doctor.

"I have heard of this Time Lord, called the Doctor—but you are not the official delegation from Gallifrey." The creature's voice now seemed to possess a more grating quality, making it painful to listen to. "I decoyed the real delegation and made them return home to Gallifrey—I could not have the Time Lords meddling in my schemes."

"And just what is your scheme, Voton?" demanded the Doctor, braving the nauseous sight before him. "Presumably you killed the Numese ambassador and took his place so you could gain entrance to the conference—but to what purpose?"

The Voton extended one of its tube-like arms and pointed it directly at the two Time Lords.

"I **shall** tell you, Doctor, but it will avail you nothing."

A fine spray emanated from a nozzle at the end of the arm and the Doctor and Romana froze solid where they stood.

"A temporary freeze-film that will render you harmless long enough for me to complete my mission, Doctor," the creature said in its rasping tone. "The Voton race has waited many lifetimes for an opportunity such as this. Members of every known species are gathered in that conference room—and when my explosive device is activated by the Vandelanian ambassador's voice frequency on the translator relay this afternoon, its reverberations will echo round the universe. Everyone will accuse everyone else of sabotage and murder. Inter-galactic warfare will break out, devastation will be immense, and when they have all weakened each other to the point of extinction, the Voton Warrior Race will rise to seize the reins of power. The Time Lords will not dare alter things on such a scale, and the Votons will be supreme! Farewell, Doctor, you and your fellow Time Lord have failed, failed, failed!!!"

Romana and the Doctor spent an anxious hour before K-9 suc-

ceeded in opening the outer door and deactivating the freeze-film. The Voton was nowhere to be seen.

"I did as you said, Master, and followed you without being seen or heard," said K-9.

"Excellent, K-9, remind me to give you a bone when we get back to the **Tardis**," congratulated the Doctor.

"Bone, Master? Please explain significance of—"

"Later, K-9," clipped the Doctor. "There isn't a moment to lose. Romana, if you go next door you'll probably find a Voton transmogrifier—they use it to change their appearance. The Voton seemed to be having trouble maintaining its Numese form, so chances are it may have to return to regenerate itself before it escapes. It won't risk staying as a Voton since they're a known enemy of the Inter-Galactic Federation. Just de-activate it somehow."

The Doctor turned to K-9. "Don't let anything through this door after I've gone, all right?"

"Affirmative, Master. They shall not pass."

"Spoken like a trooper."

Romana caught the Doctor by the arm as he was leaving.

"How will you stop the Voton, Doctor?"

"With a few well chosen words. Wish me luck."

The conference room was arranging itself into some kind of order ready for the afternoon's session as the Doctor strode in and made his way to the Chairman's platform. Without a moment's hesitation, he climbed up on the table and stamped his foot to quieten the delegates. Shocked faces greeted his unethical entrance, and a rumble of dissent buzzed round the room.

The Doctor caught sight of the livid eyes of the fake Numese delegate and launched into his hastily prepared speech.

"Madam Chairman, fellow beings, unaccustomed as I am to public speaking, I should like to seize this opportunity to say my piece before the Vandelanian ambassador begins his address."

"Sit down at once," exhorted the Chairman, "you will have your chance to speak later. Please observe the conference protocol. Even Time Lords must show a proper sense of decency."

The Doctor turned on her angrily, his eyes flaring.

"Decency?! Remain silent so that those microscopic bugs up there can dictate what we can and can't do in our own universe?"

A gasp of horror went up from the assembled delegates.

"They claim our investigation into their life-style and civilisation is an intrusion on their privacy. How dare they say such a blasphemous thing? By what right are they inviolate from scientific research? That a lower order of life, a race of creeping vermin should tell us what to do is unthinkable!"

By now there was uproar from the outraged conference as delegates stood and jeered the Doctor's words, but he continued unabashed.

"What is our answer to this impertinence? I say let us abandon our research into such insignificant species. Instead we should exterminate them like the bacteria they are, grind them under our heels and be done with them!"

The cacophony of angry voices continued unabated for several minutes while the Doctor was dragged from the platform. At length the conference room was stilled and the Vandelanian ambassador rose to speak.

"Grovelling, filthy germ!" shouted the Doctor as he stood, held tightly by two security guards.

The Vandelanian ambassador seethed with anger. A high-pitched squeal burst forth from him as he poured a tirade of invective on the Doctor, who stood smiling and goading him on with further insults.

"Remove the Time Lord from the conference room," commanded the Chairman. "You are a disgrace to Gallifrey and this Federation. What reason you could possibly have—"

"There!" shouted the Doctor, pointing at the Numese mud-creature, whose form in the last few minutes had become increasingly unstable. "That's the reason —he's a Voton agent who murdered the Numese ambassador and has set an explosive device to destroy this conference room and everyone in it."

It took only a fraction of a second for the delegates to realise the truth of the Doctor's accusations. By the time the Voton was finally overpowered, any semblance of disguise had faded, and the creature was once more its repugnant self.

The Doctor, meanwhile, had felt it wise to make himself scarce after his inflammatory speech. From the safety of the **Tardis,** he, Romana and K-9, watched the closing of the conference by patching the **Tardis** screen into the building's video system.

The Chairman was making her final address, her slender form perfectly poised on her three slim legs as her triple-mouth spoke the words in three languages simultaneously.

" . . . and finally we must thank the delegate from Gallifrey for unmasking the enemy in our midst, despite his rather unorthodox methods, which I'm sure our sub-microscopic colleagues will forgive in the circumstances."

The Doctor looked rather pleased with himself.

"I think I made rather a hit there. If I hadn't angered the ambassador and made him raise his voice two octaves we'd have all gone boom. A touch of genius, though I say so myself—"

"Doctor," Romana said quietly, drawing his attention back to the screen.

The small figure of Meristan, the security official, stood dwarfed by the Chairman on the platform, as she continued her vote of thanks.

" . . . he was, of course, not to know that Meristan here had already spotted the device implanted in the micro-autoling circuits and rendered it harmless, before surrounding the conference room with a security ring."

"Oh no," groaned the Doctor, switching off the screen. "To think I went through all that for nothing; I should have guessed—it did make me wonder why the Voton was happily sitting there waiting to get blown up with the rest of us."

"It just goes to show that history can sometimes look after itself without your help, Doctor," commented Romana, hiding a smile.

"And I missed hearing the speech as well," the Doctor suddenly realised. Then his eyes brightened. "Never mind. I'll reset the controls and we'll go back a couple of hours and try again."

Romana stepped in between him and the console. "Oh no, you don't, Doctor. This is a democratic ship and K-9 and I say no, don't we, K-9?"

"Affirmative, Mistress. Power to the people."

"And computerised dogs," added Romana, with a grin.

SPACE FACTS

Things every would-be space traveller should know about the fascinating world of the stars . . .

A Armstrong, Neil. The first man on the moon, stepping down on to the Sea of Tranquillity from Apollo 11 on July 20, 1969.

B Booster. Powerful thrust engines used to boost spacecraft into orbit, then jettisoned and recovered by parachute.

C Crab Nebula. 'Exploding star', one of a group of stars called supernovae, emitting radio waves and X-rays.

D Dish. Another term for the paraboloid on a radio telescope. The dish swings round and tilts, collecting signals from space.

E Eclipse. When the moon passes over the face of the sun. When this happens the sun's corona can be seen clearly—the corona is a pale halo of gases around the sun, invisible most of the time.

F Fra Mauro. Area of the moon south of the Apollo 12 landing-site in 1970. The Apollo 13 mission, later the same year, attempted to reach Fra Mauro but was unsuccessful.

G Galaxy. Earth is just part of one of the many galaxies in space, made up of millions of planets, moons and suns. Earth is on the edge of our galaxy, about 30,000 light years from the centre.

H Halley's Comet. A famous comet appearing over Britain only very rarely. Depicted in the Bayeux Tapestry, Halley's Comet has a long tail and a glowing head made up of dust, ice and rock particles. Comets travel great distances and every time they pass the sun some of their substance melts away.

I Io. One of twelve moons—Io, Europa, Ganymede and Callisto are the largest—circling the planet Jupiter. The moons were discovered by Galileo in 1610.

J Jodrell Bank. A famous radio telescope in Cheshire, Britain, receiving signals from sources such as nebulae, interstellar gas clouds and quasars. The first radio telescope was invented by an American, J.C. Jansky, in 1931.

K Kagoshima Space Centre. Japan became the world's fourth space power when it launched its first satellite, Osumi, from this site in 1970.

L Lunar Roving Vehicle (LRV). First used on the moon during Apollo 15, in 1971. Modified car or jeep used for moving on the moon and carrying heavy rock samples.

M Mars. Called the 'red' planet because of its red-looking deserts, Mars is about half the size of Earth, and is unfit for humans to live on as the atmosphere contains carbon dioxide.

N Neptune. Discovered in 1846, Neptune is much larger than Earth and has two moons. The temperature is very cold all the time, and the atmosphere is frozen at -220°C.

O Ocean of Storms. Surveyors 1 and 3 landed here on the nearside of the moon in the years before a moon landing was attempted. These probes sent back thousands of valuable photos of the moon. Later Apollo 12 landed there in 1969 and set up a research station.

P Pulsating Universe Theory. This theory tries to explain the nature of the universe and assumes that the universe is alternately expanding and contracting. When the limit is reached, the galaxies will be squeezed tightly together and there will be a cosmic explosion, so that the cycle renews itself.

Q Quasar. Astronomers are not sure what these bodies are, but they are star-like and produce radio waves and immense power. One theory believes that they are relics of old galaxies, spinning away from us on the very boundary of the universe.

R Red Spot. This is a phenomenon connected with the planet Jupiter. Gases in the clouds form blue and pink bands around the planet, and the Red Spot can be seen through a telescope—it is big enough to engulf our Earth. No one is sure why the Red Spot forms.

S Satellites. Natural or artificial, satellites circle our earth and in the case of natural satellites, circle many other planets in the galaxy. Russian and American man-made satellites collect information about our planet and space, relaying it back to us through use of radio telescopes.

T Tereshkova was the surname of the famous female astronaut Valentina Tereshkova. A Russian textile worker, she took up parachute jumping and this led her to become a cosmonaut. Her epic space flight in Vostok 6 lasted 71 hours.

U Uranus. A planet physically similar to Jupiter and Saturn, with five moons.

V Venus. One of the brightest stars in the heavens, Venus's atmosphere is mainly carbon dioxide, which retains a lot of the sun's heat.

W World System. This was a theory put forward by Ptolemy, a Greek scientist, who believed that the Earth was the centre of the Universe, flanked by the Sun and Moon. Ptolemy lived from AD 120 to AD 180.

X X-Rays. These are emitted from certain kinds of stars, called supernovae, whose collapsed bodies, after a great deal of time, become pulsars. It is these pulsars which emit X-rays and radio waves.

Y Young, John. An American astronaut who landed on the moon in 1972. His companion on the Apollo 16 mission was Charles Duke.

Z Zond. A certain type of spacecraft which, together with the Luna Orbiter and Apollo craft, succeeded in getting photographs of the far side of the moon.

Scanning the SKIES

You shouldn't have any difficulty in recognising the enormous radio telescope in our picture. It is of course the largest of three such telescopes operated by Manchester University's Nuffield Laboratories at Jodrell Bank in Cheshire.

The Nuffield Laboratories are doing fascinating and exciting research into all aspects of radio astronomy, and they are finding out a great deal about the vast reaches of space around us. The Jodrell Bank telescopes seem to be most often in the news when they are tracking space flights, but strangely enough this part of their work takes up only a small proportion of their time.

They are much more actively concerned with research into such complicated-sounding subjects as: distribution of neutral hydrogen in the Galaxy and in extragalactic nebulae; studies of radio emission from interstellar OH molecules, and polarization of the continuum radio emission from the Galaxy and of the radio emission from radio galaxies and quasars. And that's just three projects, chosen from a long list!

The staff at the Nuffield Laboratories rely to a great extent on computers to help them analyse the results they obtain from the telescopes. The largest of these, the Control Data Corporation 7600, was at the time of its installation in Manchester University the most powerful computer in the world, with an addition time of less than one microsecond.

THE QUESTION OF QUASARS

You may have noticed one interesting word in the list of research projects above: quasars. Quasars have to some extent caught the public's attention in the last few years, mainly because everyone loves a good mystery. No one really knows just what quasars are. Or, as the Nuffield Laboratories put it, 'Quasars possess physical properties which have yet to be explained.'

Quasars are strong emitters of *apparent* radio brightness, as observed from the earth, yet all the observational evidence suggests that they are extremely distant objects. This means that their *absolute* radio brightnesses are immense.

A typical quasar emits a million times more radio energy than our own Galaxy, the Milky Way, from a volume of space which is 30,000 times smaller than the Milky Way. When you consider that the Milky Way contains sufficient material to make 100,000 million stars like the Sun, you will get some idea of the mind-boggling amounts of radio energy possessed by these mysterious bodies.

Because of their great distances from us, and their compact volumes, quasars look like stars on photographic plates, and this is how they come by their name, which means 'half-stars'.

One theory about the composition of quasars is that they occur when clouds of anti-matter meet ordinary matter in space. The resulting annihilation of atoms would release enormous amounts of energy. The theory of gravitational collapse, when giant super stars collapse in on themselves, could also be made to account for the unusual properties of quasars.

Whatever the solution to the quasar riddle proves to be, it's a fair bet that this huge telescope with its far-seeing 'eye' will play a big part in unravelling the mystery, as scientists interpret the many 'messages' it receives from space.

TOMORROW'S TRAVEL

How do you get around? Do you travel by bus, train, bike, car —even plane, sometimes? The emphasis these days is on faster and faster travel; anything to cut the time taken to get from A to B. Just think, comparatively few years ago, a trip across the Atlantic Ocean to America meant a weeks-long sea voyage in a liner, yet New York is just a couple of hours away by Concorde now.

But what of the travel of the future? What surprises and innovations do the scientists and engineers have in store for us? Let's take a look at some of the possibilities which are already on the drawing boards:

BACK PACKING

With the world fuel crisis showing no signs of abating, fuel economy is of prime importance today, and will be even more important in the years to come. As fuel prices rise and oil becomes scarcer, it is quite possible that cars will be banned altogether from our city centres of the future, and it's easy to see why: they cause congestion and pollution, and are very inefficient commuter-carriers, one car often carrying just one person to and from work, when it **could** take four.

But what are the alternatives? Improved public transport systems are the obvious answer but, looking further ahead, the powered back pack is a viable alternative. Looking rather like an aqualung, the powered unit would be strapped to the body, and the commuter would be able to manoeuvre forwards, backwards, sideways—even straight up and down! The benefits in the inner cities would be enormous, each commuter travelling independently (and economically) by the most direct route from A to B. Powered by compressed gas, the packs would be economical and would cause little or no pollution, but there **is** a drawback. As yet, the power that can be harnessed in the pack would only last for a few minutes, thus making anything but the shortest journey impractical, so until scientists come up with a way of making a portable power pack that will last for a few hours the back pack idea will remain just where it is—on the drawing board.

PLUG-IN CARS

An idea that has been around for some time now—that of the electric-powered car—suffers from the same drawback as the back pack; the cars do not run for very long without having to be recharged. Batteries used to power a car will at present last long enough for a short journey only; if more batteries were carried the extra weight would only slow down the car. So what is needed is a very powerful battery that is not heavy or cumbersome, and this is what scientists are working on. Hopefully they will be able to develop a type of simple yet powerful slot-in mini-battery that could be exchanged at service stations when it runs low, in much the same way that we refill cars with petrol today.

Another possibility is that of having a conventional engine in the car for starting and accelerating, plus a back-up power unit of batteries for cruising. This idea would, of course, be more useful for motorway travelling than for use in town, where lots of stopping and starting is involved.

The shape of the car of the future will be very streamlined, with smooth design aimed at cutting down on wind resistance for better fuel economy. Did you know that an empty roof rack on today's cars adds something like 10% to fuel bills? Design is likely to resemble aircraft as much as anything else, with covered-in wheels, integral bumpers and recessed, flush-fitting headlamps.

Solar cells, now used on a small scale for heating houses and other buildings, could be positioned on the car's roof, trapping the sun's energy and using it to power the car's radio, etc.

The car's dashboard will conceal a mini-computer and the driver, at the flick of a console switch, will receive detailed information on route availability, fuel consumption, estimated time of arrival—even weather conditions he is likely to meet. The driver may also become somewhat unnecessary in the car of the future; he will simply set the car's automatic navigation system, then sit back and enjoy the trip!

TRAINS . . .

Trains have two big plusses going for them: they cause little or no pollution, and their safety record is enviable. Also, travelling on their own routes they cause no traffic congestion and don't clog up the inner cities as buses and cars do.

Most trains of the future will be powered by electricity, but there are also plans to produce new types of coal-powered trains, too. Not the old steam engines, of course, but new engines based on a method of burning coal so that it gives off little or no pollution, but lots of heat. Crushed coal is fed into an enclosed furnace on the train, and water in a boiler is heated. The steam generated powers turbines which in turn power electric motors, propelling the train at great speeds. Coal has a good future as a fuel—we should have more than enough for the next thousand years or so.

The trains that run under ground (like the London Underground system) also have a future, but not in covering the small inner-city areas that they traverse today. The underground trains of the future would run many hundreds of metres below the surface, and would transport passengers and cargo for hundreds and hundreds of miles in vacuum-filled tunnels at speeds of up to 10,000 kph!

Back on the earth's surface, hover-trains may appear, running on a metal track, suspended just above it by a magnetic field. They would be economical to run, powered by a linear electric motor, and could reach speeds in excess of 600 kph.

. . . AND BOATS

When you realise that some two thirds of the earth's surface is covered by water, it is obvious that, with man's ever-growing population and thirst for resources, the seas will be of great importance in the future.

Underwater travel, by submarine, is sure to increase. Passengers and cargo will be carried by huge subs, their great advantage being that, travelling below the surface of the water, they are unhampered by currents and weather conditions. Mini-subs are being developed so that tourists can be taken to the depths of the oceans to see the marine life there and, looking further into the future, they could also be used as local transport between underwater towns and cities.

Small, fast hydrofoils are also being developed, but they have one great disadvantage: their fuel capacity is limited, so that they can only be used for relatively short journeys. One solution to this problem is to have fleets of huge submarines patrolling the oceans, which would surface on demand, enabling the hydrofoils to refuel in the middle of the ocean.

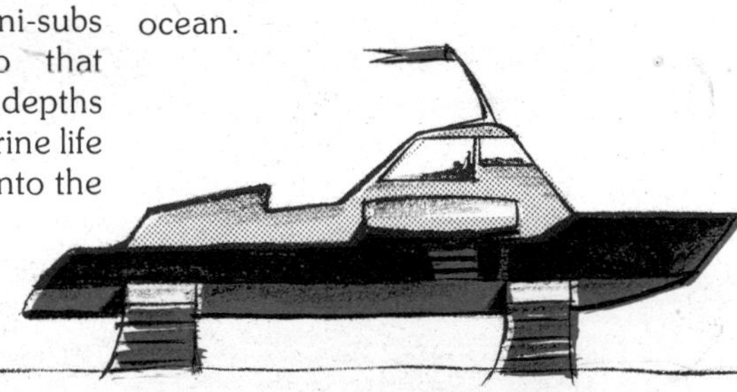

. . . AND PLANES

Big improvements in the speed and range of modern-day aircraft are technically possible—but they are proving too costly to put into practice. As in all forms of future travel, the plane's development is characterised by one thing: fuel economy. One idea is that planes should be powered by liquid hydrogen. Liquid hydrogen must be stored carefully, and takes up more storage space than petroleum-based fuels but, being obtained from water, it is very plentiful and easily available. The liquid-hydrogen fuelled planes would be enormous, and could travel at three times the speed of sound. To eliminate the problem of sonic boom, it is planned that they would fly so high that, by the time the boom reached the ground, it would have dissipated.

Airships may also make a come-back in the future. After the disasters which befell the airships or dirigibles in the late 1930s their design was discontinued, and they seemed relegated to the history books. But the highly-inflammable hydrogen that powered the old airships has now been replaced with helium, a safer, non-inflammable gas, making the whole concept of the airship a safe and attractive one once more.

The great size of the airship is one of its attractions, plus the fact that it can be used as a bulky cargo-carrier even in the underdeveloped countries, since it requires only a landing stage, not long runways.

An even more revolutionary idea is to develop airships that would be powered by the sun. Solar cells would be built into the airship's immense frame, and would convert the sun's energy into electricity to power the ship. This idea could, of course, only be put into practice in areas of the world where strong sunlight is plentiful.

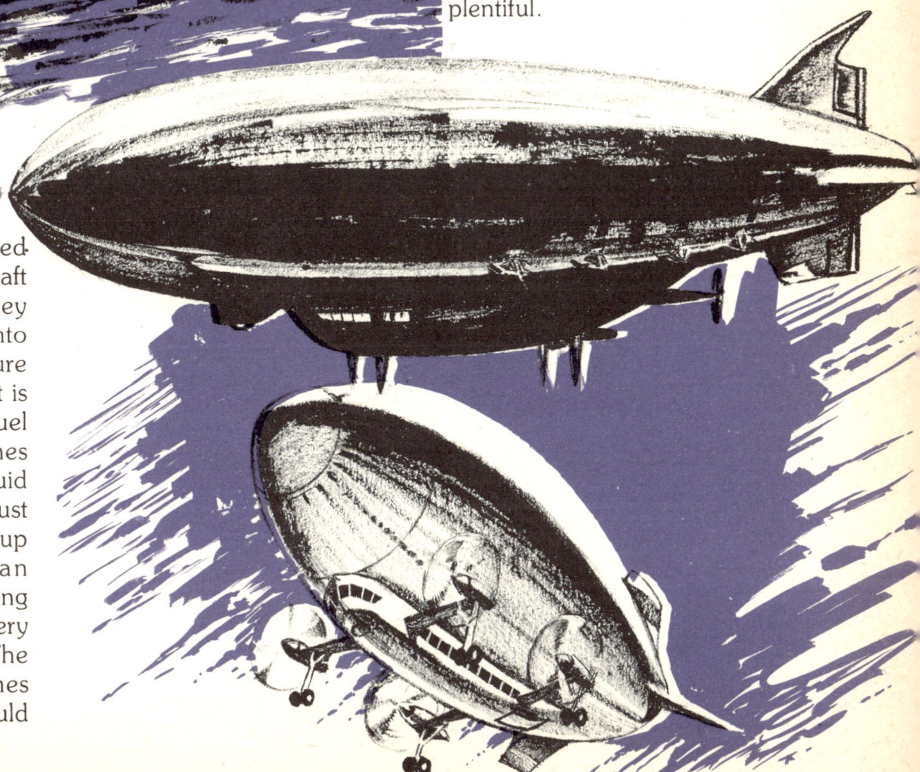

the Dogon and the white dwarf

—a possible argument for ancient astronauts and alien life?

In recent years there have been a number of legends and stories put forward as evidence for the existence of extraterrestrial life, and these have led to the various 'ancient astronaut' theories of writers like Erich von Däniken.

While none of these are detailed enough or of sufficient accuracy to be at all conclusive in proving that our own planet has at some time been visited by aliens, there is one story in particular that is still attracting the attention of astronomers and cosmologists alike. This is the Dogon myth concerning the dog-star, Sirius, which is the brightest star in our skies.

The Dogon people are a primitive, prescientific society of West Africa, who now number only a few hundred thousand, and of whom sociological studies have been carried out only since the 1930s. One of the anthropologists who studied them at that time, a Frenchman named Griaule, has recounted at some length the folklore and beliefs of the Dogon, which—as with the mythologies of many ancient civilisations—is heavily based on astronomy.

The first surprising fact was that the Dogon people believed that all the planets of our solar system rotated about their own axes, as well as revolving around the sun: also that the planets moved in elliptical rather than circular orbits.

Although these facts have now been proved scientifically, and are fairly easy to verify, they did not usually figure in the beliefs held by primitive peoples, who more often had a rather simplistic—and incorrect—view of the universe.

More surprising still, however, are Dogon beliefs that Jupiter has four satellites, and that Saturn is encircled by a ring. For it is difficult to see how they could have discovered these facts for themselves without the use of a strong astronomical telescope.

But most surprising of all is their belief regarding Sirius, the star around which their mythology is centred. For they hold that Sirius has a dark, invisible companion star which orbits it once every fifty years, and which is small but heavy, being made of a metal called *Sagala*, a very dense metal not found on Earth.

Remarkably enough, it is now known that Sirius does indeed have a strange, dark companion, and that this smaller star has a period of just 50.04 ± 0.09 years (by astronomical calculation). Furthermore, its matter is in a state never found on Earth, that known as relativistically degenerate, and this state (where electrons are not tied to the nucleus) is similar to that of metallic matter. Such a star is now known as a *white dwarf* star, and is characteristically small but dense.

So the Dogon myth is found to be backed up by scientific knowledge. The question is: since the dog-star's companion was the first white dwarf to be discovered—as recently as last century—how did it come to find its way into a primitive mythology?

One theory is that it was once visible, as Sirius is today, to the naked eye. For white dwarfs actually evolve (over a very long period of time) from large, luminous stars known as red giants. Some think it possible that at one time the red star might have been large enough to eclipse white Sirius, and that therefore at some time between then and now the two stars would both have been visible at once, so that their relative motion could have been seen quite clearly.

But in that case surely someone else would have noticed the phenomenon too—after all, they would have been two of the brightest stars in the sky. And yet none of the earliest astronomers mentioned this, nor that Sirius may have appeared as red in recorded time.

Perhaps then the origins of the Dogon myth might stretch back even further—as far as the earliest forms of man—the Dogon people being just one of those to whom this particular legend was handed down. But this would not explain their other beliefs: the ring of Saturn, or Jupiter's moons. To have acquired these facts, the Dogon must surely have been in contact with someone more knowledgeable than their fellow primitive man, with someone from a more advanced, technological civilisation.

Might some aliens, some ancient astronauts, have arrived long ago among the Dogon people? Having travelled through our galaxy to reach Earth, they would almost certainly have been in possession of all the relevant facts.

Although this is a strong possibility, there can be no proof. And in fact there are reasons to suspect another, rather more ordinary explanation of the Dogon myth.

The companion to Sirius was first discovered in 1844 by a German astronomer, Bessel, but the white dwarf theory did not come about until early this century, and its repercussions were still being discussed widely throughout Europe in the 1920s and 30s. It was probably in the air in France in the years immediately before Griaule set out for Africa.

Probably other anthropologists from Europe had visited the Mali region where the Dogon lived before Griaule arrived, and who is to say that one of them did not, by answering their questions, perhaps unwittingly add to the existing Dogon legend, so adapting it to include modern scientific knowledge, white dwarf and all? Perhaps, in other words, part of their myth dates only from earlier this century, and is quite European in origin.

In the end, nothing has been proved either way. And if extraterrestrial life is at some time proved to exist, there are more likely ways for this to happen.

As our radiotelescopes 'see' farther and farther into space, and as our unmanned spacecraft—which have already reached as far as Jupiter and Saturn in the shape of the Pioneer and Voyager probes—reach out more and more into the vastness of space, there must be an ever-increasing chance that some alien life will come to light.

At the same time, it seems less and less likely that it will be found within our own solar system. We may even need to look at other galaxies. Then we will need more powerful rockets, launching faster and faster spaceships. Even then we could never reach the speed of light—for, according to the theory of relativity, if a spacecraft were to be accelerated near to the speed of light, instead of the ship continuing to gain speed, it would begin to increase its mass, with the effect that, relatively speaking, time would slow down, eventually almost 'standing still'.

In fact this means that a ship would travel the same distance in 'less' time, so that in years to come we might be sending astronauts up in near-speed-of-light spacecraft, and a round trip to a star 25 light years away would take only about twelve years, in relative terms.

But this type of time/space travel is a long way off yet. For the present we will have to make do with the idea of ancient astronauts, and keep an open mind about the possibility of alien life revealing itself to us here on Earth.

SWEET FLOWER OF UTHE

The door of the **Tardis** swung open and the Doctor's curly brown hair, topped by his soft, broad-rimmed hat, came into view, his incredibly long scarf trailing its multi-colours behind him.

"Now, have I got everything? Jelly babies, dog whistle, string, light-beam, screwdriver . . . Well, come on, Romana, don't be all day!" shouted the Doctor back into the depths of the **Tardis.**

The Doctor stepped out on to the fresh green grass, breathed in the refreshing air, and squinted his eyes up at the twin suns shining down on the planet's surface.

K-9's squat metallic shape emerged from the **Tardis,** his antennae ears constantly tracking the surrounding atmosphere.

"Mistress will arrive in 26.4 seconds, Master," intoned K-9.

"What's taking her so long?" fumed the Doctor, obviously not in the best of tempers.

"Mistress is in the bathroom on Level 4, Master. It takes 26.4 seconds for a humanoid life-form to ascend to the main exit."

"Thank you, K-9, a very useful thing to—what's she doing washing her hands on Level 4? There's a perfectly—"

At that moment Romana stepped through the door of the **Tardis,** and emerged smiling into the sunshine.

"Sorry I took so long, Doctor, but—"

"Yes, I know."

K-9 piped up, "Level 4 is the only one at present with the facility of running water, Master. The Computer has closed down all similar services on other levels because—"

The Doctor threw his hands into the air. "Why does everyone keep telling me things I know? I'm well aware that the computer self-servicing section wants to run a check on all the plumbing in the **Tardis** and has thrown us out for the day so we don't get under its feet!"

Romana turned with a smile towards her fellow Time-Lord. "Cheer up, Doctor, it's a beautiful day and we're as free as the birds to do what we like. Do you know where we are, by the way?"

"Uthe 4. Pronounced 'youth', but spelt . . . er, differently," replied the Doctor.

"Correction. Uthe 3, Master."

The Doctor glowered at K-9, then picked up a stick from the ground and threw it as far as he could.

"Fetch, boy, go fetch."

"Master?" K-9 seemed decidedly puzzled.

"You heard, K-9. Go and fetch it," said the Doctor.

K-9, still confused by such an illogical action, set off across the hillside to collect the stick.

"And if you come across a Uthian Scatterbud bring that back too!" yelled the Doctor after the disappearing dog.

"What's a Uthian Scatterbud, Doctor?" asked Romana.

"Oh, it's a beautiful red flower, found only on the third planet of the Uthian star system—very rare; something to do with the atmosphere. It used to be the planet's symbol of peace once. I thought I'd take one to add to my collection," replied the Doctor, gazing round the surrounding countryside. "It's a hobby of mine."

Romana looked surprised. "I didn't know you collected flowers, Doctor."

The Doctor grinned mischievously. "I only started today, but don't tell K-9. It'll keep him busy for hours. Come on, let's explore."

The two Time Lords strode off down the hill, the Doctor's scarf flapping lazily in the breeze. As far as the eye could see, stretched long, rolling green hills dotted with patches of strange but beautiful woodland, and everywhere the scent of flowers floated through the air.

"Oh look, Doctor, isn't that beautiful!" cried Romana, as she saw a cloud of delicately tinted azure flowers some yards away, and skipped towards them.

"I see you've taken it up too," commented the Doctor with amusement, turning to look back the way they'd just come. "Better keep a bearing on the **Tardis**—we don't want to get lost. That's a Clutterhorn Stink Weed, incidentally, so I shouldn't go too close if—"

He was alone. "Romana?"

The breeze blew gently through his hair, but not another sound could be heard.

"Come on out, Romana, we're much too old to play hide and seek."

The next instant the Doctor felt the ground give way beneath his feet, and he was suddenly falling through blackness, his arms and legs brushing against smooth vertical walls, into a seemingly bottomless pit.

It was several minutes before the Doctor felt firm ground beneath his feet as he gently touched earth again.

"Quite remarkable, really quite remarkable," said the Doctor simply.

"Mind where you're treading, Doctor."

"Ah, Romana, there you are. Have you ever read **Alice in Wonderland?** She fell down a—never mind. We'd better find a way out of here." The Doctor paused in thought. "It's obviously some kind of artificial shaft, with these smooth walls, and nobody builds a hole this deep and instals an anti-gravity mechanism unless it leads somewhere when you get to the bottom."

"And if there's a way down—"

"Quite. So let's see if we can find a door. Ah, the very thing," said the Doctor, rummaging in his pockets and producing a compact lightbeam which instantly illuminated the space they were in. They looked round and within seconds located what seemed to be a grid, low down on the wall.

"It appears not to have been used for many years," observed Romana, pulling vainly at the rusted grating.

"Probably a left-over from the Uthian global war last century. Totally destroyed four-fifths of the planet," explained the Doctor. "It was the most complete example of a race committing suicide." He wrestled with the grating.

"There were no survivors?" asked Romana, horrified.

"Nobody was ever found alive, that's for sure," answered the Doctor, panting heavily with the exertion.

"But why does nobody live here now? It's a beautiful place," countered Romana. "They're not afraid of ghosts?"

"No, no, of course not," responded the Doctor. "It was decided to leave the planet as a monument to peace, a sort of warning to other races." The grid finally came away in his hands. "There we are. Come on, Romana, there has to be a way out somewhere along here."

The Doctor lowered himself through the hole and helped Romana down. They found themselves in a dark and decaying

corridor which, despite a century of disuse, was still remarkably intact.

"Eeny, meeny, miny . . . mo. This way," cried the Doctor emphatically, and set off at an energetic pace, the light-beam sweeping along the floor in front of him.

After a few moments, however, his finger went suddenly up to his lips. "Ssssh, Romana," he began quietly. "There's a light down there. Look."

Sure enough they could see in the distance a narrow block of light appearing. The faint sound of an electronic siren reached their ears, and soon the patter of feet and a collection of dancing pinpricks of light could be seen approaching them along the corridor.

"I'm not sure we ought to wait and meet whatever it is," suggested Romana, pulling the Doctor in the opposite direction.

"Discretion **is** the better part of valour," agreed the Doctor, and together they raced off, away from the advancing lights.

A searing beam of red luminescence crashed into the wall just in front of them, and an imperious voice boomed through the semi-darkness.

"Stay exactly where you are or I shall be forced to kill you."

"Ever had an offer you can't refuse?" asked the Doctor, softly.

The group of figures quickly surrounded them in an escort, their weapons raised in warning. They were dressed in cleanly cut, black military uniforms, the design of a scatterbud clearly visible on their helmets.

The one who had fired the warning shot, and was obviously an officer, took in the situation immediately.

"You three repair that damage at once. We don't want the Rad-Plague leaking in from the upper levels." He surveyed the Doctor and Romana critically. "The Supreme Commander will want to see you two in the Control Centre."

"Oh good," said the Doctor. "Will you take us to your leader?"

The slab-like, reinforced doors to the Control Centre slid open with a swift hiss as the officer pressed his palm against the ident-pad on the wall. The Doctor and Romana found themselves in a large, dome-shaped room, dominated by an imposing three-dimensional model of one of the continents of Uthe, which stood in the centre of the floor. Coloured pieces dotted the miniature landscape, a microcosm of some gargantuan struggle between two opposing armies. Surveying the battlefield, his face a study of deep concentration, the Supreme Commander barely noticed the strangers' entrance.

"Have the autofacs in sectors 4 and 7 switch to production of DRK Rapier Night-Fighter robots until further notice," he snapped to the programmer seated at the computer console.

"Supreme Commander?" The officer stepped forward to present his prisoners, saluting smartly as his superior paused in his strategising and turned to discover the cause of this interruption.

"Ah, the spies," he said menacingly, and beckoned the Doctor and Romana forward. "This is what you wanted to see, my friends. Look your last upon our battle plans, for I fear you will not live to pass on the information to our enemies."

The Doctor peered intently at the model before him. "An interesting position," he observed, thoughtfully. "Don't you think your left flank is a little exposed? I mean, if the enemy were to swing round in an arc here, instead of pushing forward as you clearly expect them to, you advance positions would be cut off without support."

"What?" asked the Supreme Commander, taken aback.

"Believe me, I've seen a few battles in my time . . . Waterloo, the Tambon Moon massacre, the conquest of Vitulbray. Now if you move your laser-missile banks from here to here," continued the Doctor calmly, "they wouldn't dare try anything so foolhardy. May I?"

The Doctor reached forward to move one of the pieces, but the Supreme Commander's baton came down and rapped him sharply on the wrist.

"Oh well, if you don't want me to play, I'll keep my suggestions to myself," said the Doctor, rubbing his arm ruefully. "I was only trying to be helpful. But it is **your** game after all."

"Game!" roared the Commander. "Game? War is not a game, sir! War means the destruction of millions of credits' worth of highly sophisticated robots and military technology, the lives of innocent populations—"

"In that order of importance, I presume," commented the Doctor, wryly.

The Commander's voice turned to ice. "Do not anger me needlessly, sir. Your life is already forfeit, but I can make your interrogation a great deal slower and more painful."

The Doctor smiled and walked casually around the perimeter of the board, drumming his fingers along the edges.

"I have one piece of information that would solve all your problems at a stroke." He paused to let the words take effect, then stepped back to address the room as a whole. "Ladies, gentlemen, your attention, please."

The technicians and military personnel momentarily paused in their tasks and turned to look at this incongruous figure who disturbed their duties.

"My name's the Doctor, good evening," he began, clearing his throat. "It is my great pleasure to inform you that all hostilities have now ceased. In fact, the planet of Uthe is at peace, and has been for the last 127 years."

If he had suddenly decided to do a tap-dance on top of the strategy board, the Doctor could not have caused a more dramatic reaction. The room was full of murmurings.

"Peace!?" bellowed the Commander, silencing everyone. "The man's insane. Even now, across the radioactive continents of Uthe, littered with their devastated cities, the armies of the enemy are gathering to hurl themselves into the final onslaught."

Romana laughed quietly. "Radioactive continents? Your computer must be seriously malfunctioning. Your planet's surface is green and luxuriant with life—the war is long over, Commander. The enemy no longer exists."

A swift blow felled Romana, and powerful arms restrained the Doctor as he leapt to her defence.

The Supreme Commander fumed with rage. "Take them from my sight!"

The two Time Lords were bundled out of the room unceremoniously by the guards, and the great doors hissed shut with a metallic clang.

"You would have thought he'd have welcomed a little advice," said the Doctor. "Some people take game playing far too seriously."

The room was crowded. The Doctor and Romana picked themselves up from the floor and secured a space against the wall next to a group of fellow prisoners.

"Is that Supreme Commander really serious, Doctor? Does he believe he's fighting a war that's happening now, right this minute, on the surface?" asked Romana, disbelievingly.

"They were—or should I say, the Uthians **are** a very stubborn race, not very imaginative but terribly persevering," replied the Doctor.

"They'd have to be," commented Romana. "Presumably they must have stayed down here, lived and died here for generations. But what I don't understand is why they believe the war is still going on. Why don't they go up and look for themsevles?"

"Pardon my overhearing you, comrades," a prisoner next to them said suddenly. "My name's Troy, Commander Troy, late of the Military Control Staff. You've just been caught?"

"Yes. I'm the Doctor, and this is Romana, my companion. What are you in here for, Troy?"

"Same as you from what you were saying. All of us here have attempted to reach the surface. We want peace; after two centuries of warfare there are many who feel this way. All our attempts to send secret peace envoys to the surface have failed however. Most of us have been imprisoned here, as you see, but the others—so we are told—have fallen victims to the Rad-Plague."

"Rad-Plague?" queried the Doctor. "The officer mentioned that earlier."

"You've not heard of it?" said Troy, surprised. "The Computer tells us it covers the whole planet surface now. Nothing can live up there without protection, which is why the armies are all robot troops. Even so, all of us are willing to die in an attempt to reach the enemy war centres and offer them peace terms."

The Doctor restrained Romana from saying anything, and leant forward close to Troy's face.

"Tell me, Troy, what part does the Computer play in this war?"

"It **is** the war, Doctor. It relays all the battle information from the surface, and transmits all our orders to our robot forces. There are many, similar computer-operated war centres buried deep beneath the surface all over the planet. They were specially designed to wage war—"

"And little else, I imagine," mused the Doctor. "I wonder . . . ."

The door flew open before the Doctor could voice his thoughts aloud, and two guards roughly dragged him to his feet.

"I rather think the Commander wants my advice after all," he cried over his shoulder. "Don't wait up for me!"

The situation on the strategy board had changed considerably. A tide of blue pieces had swept across it, and were now threatening to engulf the beleagured black forces. The Supreme Commander looked both worried and angry.

"Now tell me, Doctor. The enemy is using some new and deadly secret weapon. My forces cannot hold them back. What is it?"

"I think you'd probably call it cheating," replied the Doctor, calmly. "If I might have a word with your computer I think I can take care of it. May I? I rather think at this stage of the game you have very little to lose and everything to gain by letting me help. Don't you?"

The Commander's brow wrinkled in momentary indecision. "Very well," he said at last. "But kill him if he makes a false move," he ordered his guards.

"So kind," said the Doctor and moved to the console. "Ah, an FL 400 Series D. Quite advanced of its kind. Now let me see. What does this button do?"

He depressed a button on the console and sat back, one hand across his mouth as he let out a long, low exhalation of breath.

"That's the external communicator—he's giving our position away to the troops immediately above us!" yelled the programmer.

"I never said a word; did you see my lips move?" protested the Doctor. "You'll forgive me if I'm a little slow with the controls. It's 160 years or more since I saw one of these. Ah, this is the one!"

An opaque, white sphere above the console began to glow.

"You must be the Computer," said the Doctor cheerily. "How do you do? Having fun are we?"

"The war progresses satisfactorily."

"Hardly. These chaps are losing and you're supposed to be on their side, aren't you?" The Doctor paused. "Except you're not, are you?"

"What do you mean by that?"

"You're a war computer," continued the Doctor. "The only thing you know how to do is wage war. When everything on the surface was finally obliterated 127 years ago, you got a bit confused, didn't you? And rather than spoil your fun, you decided not to tell anyone."

"It is a lie. The war has never stopped."

"Don't tell lies now, there's a good computer. You continued the war on an imaginary basis and fed all these unfortunate people false information for over a century—false statistics, false troop movements, false war material production figures, false pictures supposedly taken of surface battles. It's all an illusion created by you, isn't it?"

"This man must be destroyed. He is an enemy spy who seeks to undermine our war effort. Destroy him! Destroy him now!"

The Doctor held up his hand to the assembled crowd of personnel. "Let's not be too hasty. What would you say if I could prove it?"

"You cannot."

The Doctor sat back in his chair, arms behind his head in a relaxed pose. "Tell me, Computer, how would you describe conditions on the surface at this moment—with particular reference to natural life-forms?"

"The surface is a barren, dead landscape devoid of all life. Nothing natural could survive the Rad-Plague."

A metallic clang on the Control Centre doors made everyone turn their heads. The Doctor smiled, a twinkle of confidence in his eyes.

"That will be for me—will you let him in? And don't worry—he's perfectly harmless."

The Commander nodded and the doors opened to reveal K-9 standing outside.

"I have your Uthanian Scatter-bud, Master."

"Good boy, K-9, very good boy."

The Doctor held the deep, red blossom up to the console screen.

"What about this? Do you know where it grows, Computer? The only place it can grow, in fact?"

A high-pitched whine was suddenly emitted from the console, and around the room several banks of equipment short-circuited with a din of electronic crackling and smoke. The Doctor turned to face the amazed onlookers.

"This, ladies and gentlemen, as I'm sure you've realised, is the sweet flower of Uthe, the scatter-bud, which flowers only on the planet Uthe 3—your planet. If you would kindly release the prisoners and my companion, I'm sure my friend K-9 will show us a way up to the surface."

"It would be impossible to thank you enough, Doctor and Romana," said Troy, as they stood outside the **Tardis** some time later. "You have freed my people from two centuries of slavery to war. How can we ever repay you?"

The Doctor grinned shrewdly. "By keeping this planet as beautiful and peaceful as it is now."

"Indeed we will, Doctor," replied Troy. "This has been the war to end all war."

"I think I've heard that somewhere before, but never mind. If you can persevere in war, I'm sure you can use your talents to make a new beginning for your race. There will be others, like yourselves, whose lives have been ruled by these war computers. You must seek them out and release them." The Doctor looked at Romana. "Well, we must be off or we'll be late for tea. Goodbye and good luck."

"Ah tea!" beamed the Doctor, "Nectar of the Gods."

"How did you do it, Doctor—get K-9 to appear at such a timely moment?"

The Doctor took a sip from his steaming cup. "I simply opened the external communications channel and used my secret weapon," he said, smiling. "I knew K-9 would have found the flower, and that was all the proof I needed to defeat the computer—an undeniable proof that the surface was capable of sustaining life, and not a dead planet as the computer maintained."

"But what was your secret weapon?"

"All I had to do was whistle. You know how to whistle, don't you?" The Doctor opened his hand to reveal the ultra-sonic dog whistle, and the control room filled with the laughter of the two Time Lords, as the **Tardis** dematerialised and set forth on new adventures.

THE CENTOVIAN PROBLEM